SOLID MAGIC

BY TAGENAR

Solid Magic
Copyright © 2021 by Tagenar

This is a work of fiction. All characters and events are products of the author's imagination. Any resemblance to real persons or events is coincidence. Except for the Netherworld. That is a real place, so do not search for it. Should you find a passageway, do not enter. There are no muscular dragon husbands over there.

Editing by **Ian Madison Keller**, MadisonKeller.net

Published by KTM Publishing

Print edition set in Fanwood, and Yellow Magician, both royalty-free typefaces

Print edition ISBN: 978-1-7322824-8-3

SESSION 1

I guess I have to trust all of you. I never did learn how to read or write, and I have no reason to start now. You really are writing down everything I say as I say it? That's hard for me to imagine. Funny it sounds impossible, since I've lived so many impossible things in my life. Everything I've done in the last forty years has been impossible, so why can't I imagine being able to write as fast as a person talks?

Scribe's shorthand? Eighty years and I've never heard of it.

Thanks for the chair. Most of them can't hold my weight, so this is definitely one of the chairs from a mansion somewhere. Where did you find this? A donation from the House of Terend. How generous. Nice to know I didn't make an enemy out of everyone. It's a custom-made chair built to hold a dragon in an eight-foot-tall man's body. It's designed to let me spread my arms and legs so my muscles don't bunch together too obscenely. I remember years ago telling someone I liked how their design felt on my scales. Something about the polish and fabric they used. Next thing I knew, all the noble houses had a chair like this. One reserved just for me in case I stopped by. Almost a throne, but unlike the monarchs, I fill the chair. Yes, thank you. I'm glad I'll be comfortable.

Well, here goes. I used to be a mercenary. Hired sword, I guess they're calling it now. My parents were merchants, trading in crafts made by other people, but I didn't care about that shit. As soon as I was old enough to be on my own, I left. Got odd jobs here and there and finally got in with a group of mercenaries. They trained me to be a hired sword, doing the covert stuff kingdoms wouldn't trust one of their own to do, or just didn't want to get their hands dirty in case something went wrong.

That's really all I did. Transport secret documents between kingdoms, slaughter a guard or two so the real soldiers could get into a fortress. It paid well enough, and I seemed to be good at it. I preferred combat only when I myself wasn't in danger of being in combat.

Must have done that from age thirteen until age thirty-eight. Just after that winter was when the court wizard of the Hirinda kingdom—queendom? Is that right? Doesn't sound right to call it a kingdom when there's no king on the throne.[1] Domain? Realm? Sorry.

My name used to be Michael Ferrante, son of Albert Ferrante and Michelle Despoe. Merchants in the northern kingdoms. They had four children. I was the only one to leave home, from what I hear. I don't know where they are now or how they're doing, and I didn't care until now, I guess. Now that I can't go home, I want to. I don't have any feelings of attachment or anything. I just keep wondering if they ever knew what happened to me. If they ever saw me like this and realized who I was.

Before I came along, the nine kingdoms did not get along. Each was its own separate country, and they did not cooperate for anything. Things sure are different now, and I don't like the direction they're heading. So much has happened that I don't even believe I have to get someone to write it all down. Hope you're not squeamish, because I'm giving details.

---

1 *Scribe's Note: At this moment, we requested he refrain from digressions to ensure accuracy.*

Sometime after my thirty-eighth winter, I was staying at an inn in the Hirinda kingdom. A queen named Unari sat on the throne back then. I forget how she was related to all the other noble families, but she had only been on the throne for about six years and she made her priorities clear: she loved the mystic arts, and she gave lots and lots of patronage to the mages. Wizards and witches migrated to the Hirinda kingdom in caravans—I wouldn't sell you water[2]—in the hopes they would find funding for their craft.

By the time I wandered that far from home, the queen had been on the throne for four years. I had been hired to fetch this magical ingredient or that magical ore since the week I arrived, and I was doing well enough to buy a house by that point, but I held back, expecting it wouldn't last forever. It couldn't. Was too good to last long, having work all the time, being in demand, not having to travel for weeks at a time before finding work.

That's when I met her. Era. Not her birth name—she got it when she was initiated into the mage guild. Wanted to move on from her old life, and I don't blame her. She walked in and came straight to me. I wasn't much of a drinker, but I did enjoy this tavern's cider, and I had a pint next to me along with a cut of venison. I will never forget what she said as she took a seat in front of me.

"Whatever your usual fee is, I'm willing to pay double for this task."

For the first time in my life, money didn't motivate me. I asked her to go on.

"There's a dragon in a cave a few days south of here. We need someone to test a new weapon on it. Killing the dragon is not necessary. We only need a report on how well the weapon performs."

---

2 SCHOLAR'S NOTE: An expression meaning "I wouldn't deceive you," often used in a joking manner.

I was dumbfounded. Double my fee, and I don't even have to kill the damn thing? Only the craziest bastards[3] would dare go near a dragon, and if I understood what she was asking, I only had to poke it and run. I wasn't even drunk and I said I was interested.

Next thing I knew, I was being escorted to the castle. I didn't meet the queen, but that's when I started to get the feeling the queen was quite the patron of the magic arts. Research into magic was flourishing under her reign. Now it makes sense, but back then I hadn't made the connection between all the magic I was seeing around me and the new monarch. I really didn't give much thought to the bigger picture back then, especially when it came to politics and marriage and noble families. I preferred to stay as far away from the nobility as possible.

Let me tell me something about the noble families. They want you to respect their grand lineage and the accomplishments of their ancestors, but all they do is sit on their asses and charge the people to live on the land they own. That's it. They're the only people legally allowed to own land—the very people who got the monarchy to pass decrees forbidding anyone to own land except for themselves—and then they look down their noses on everyone else for being poor and having no land of their own. They'll tell you their bloodline is pure, so that's why they deserve to own the land and their subjects surrender a third of their harvest every year, or pay them a tax to hunt deer in the forests their family owns. They want everyone to believe the aristocrats are the best people in society because they have money and land and their ancestors were brave on the battlefield, but all they do is gossip about each other and complain about all the poor people in the country. After

---

3 Some manuscripts replace this word with a vulgar slang term for a snake, likely a change in the thirteenth century to avoid offending Joseph the Bastard, who briefly united five of the kingdoms under his rule.

taking a cut of the harvest as tribute, they throw people in jail for trying to hunt deer, conscript farmer's children to fight the wars they start—all to prove they deserve their station—yes, they start wars just to prove they can command people to victory, and that justifies everything they do in their minds—and then they complain about all these hungry people everywhere who toil in the dirt and wonder why they resent the nobility.

I didn't really see it that way at the time, though. All I knew was that if you didn't lick their boots just right, they'd fuck your life up worse than a bear. Saw it happen a few times. Man turned his back on a nobleman's wife, she had him locked up and flogged. I was the one who got on my knees and begged forgiveness on his behalf. So yes, I just left them alone.

Now here I was in the arcane chambers. I was staring at a sword, and Era was telling me they had to perform a ritual to bind me to this magical weapon. A few chants and sparks later, I felt something. Like an invisible rope tying me to this sword, and then something strange happened. The sword began to change shape. Before, it had been just a standard blade, but after the chanting stopped, it changed into something else. The blade curved and gained a serrated edge. It looked like the kind of sword I had always wanted, if I'd ever wanted to spend money on something as luxurious and impractical as a sword. Impractical for my line of work, I mean. I couldn't believe it. It was my sword. The one I had always imagined. I watched it become that before my eyes, and when I picked it up, I felt complete.

Era told me the sword was magically bound to me, and it would become whatever I needed it to be. It was an experimental form of magic, so its effects had not been fully studied. It had won me over right then. It was too heavy when I picked it up, so it became lighter. The serrated parts of the blade were too large, so as I held it, they became finer, almost too fine to see.

And *they* were paying *me* to wield this thing?

I had a feeling something was wrong. The weapon didn't feel like metal. It didn't feel like it belonged here. Like, I was holding it, but it wasn't normal. What's the word? It felt like it existed somewhere else, far away, and yet I was still holding it. It scribbled me up,[4] but I went along with it anyway. It was just another magical job. It stood out, but I didn't think it was strange enough to back out. In fact, I was curious. Yes, for the first time in my life, I think I took a job out of curiosity. It's what happens when money doesn't motivate you.

Era paid me half up front. I had a map to the dragon's cave, and Era claimed to be able to tell from the sword itself if I had done the job or was just making it up. I believed her, and I intended to follow through. These mages were fucking rich, and I wanted them to hire me again. I didn't have any magical talent myself, and I had sure tried, but I was useful to them for fetching things they needed from the far reaches of the realm. Just a nick on the leg or something, and then sprint back home, though the more nicks the better, she said.

They offered to hold my knives for me while I was gone, but I kept them as a precaution. I had never carried a sword before; too bulky and heavy for my kind of work, so I expected this would be a change of pace. Just as I thought that, the sword shrank into a knife-sized version of itself, and it fit into one of the holsters I already had strapped to my belt. I was dumbfounded, but I left that knife with

---

4 An expression meaning "gave me the creeps," after the rumor that all scribes were part of some sort of secret society bent on overthrowing monarchs and establishing a single kingdom under their control, a fearsome notion at the time. Here, M is making a deliberate tongue-in-cheek jab at the scribes in attendance.

them. There was a time in my younger days I would have been tempted to sell such a weapon and flee to another kingdom, but this thing scared me. If the mages could make something that did this, I didn't want to find out what they would do if I crossed them.

The path I had to follow would take me eight days walking, and I had enough supplies to last me that long. Era told me I had to avoid all other magic sources while carrying the sword, so I couldn't risk taking carriages or meeting anybody else along the way. Something about it affecting the new magic. These people were doing serious research under the queen, so I planned to follow their instructions exactly.

I remember it being sunny most of the way, even staying off the paths and cutting my own trails through the underbrush. I had to climb a few trees to see the stars and get my bearings. When I set down for the night, I passed the time playing with the sword. I imagined the blade was longer, and it became longer. I imagined it as a pitchfork, and it stretched and separated into three prongs.

I spent hours changing it into various pieces of cutlery, and then on a whim I pictured it made of wood. The sword shrank and thickened into a small wooden sword, the kind every carpenter makes for the children with the leftover scraps of whatever project. It even had a wooden hilt. That's when I realized it looked exactly like the one I remember playing with as a child. Same size, too. That thought took me back to the many times I hit my brothers with it, and the many times they smacked me with theirs. As a kid I had wished for these things to be smoother so we wouldn't get splinters. The sword became like glass in my hand. Wooden glass. Polished like a nobleman's table.

Over the next few days, I got to know this weapon extremely well. It was like I was figuring out how to talk to it, and it was figuring out what I wanted. The bond was strange. A rope tying me to the sword. Even when I let go of it, I felt I was still holding it. I tested it a few nights. I set it on the ground and walked away from it. Sure enough, the farther away I went, the more I felt like I was leaving a piece of myself behind. At five yards, it was just a vague feeling of unease. Fifty yards and I was starting to feel sick. A hundred yards and I could barely breathe. Twenty more yards and I slipped and fell. It was as if the sword had yanked the rope and was pulling me backwards. I had to crawl back it hurt so much.

I'd heard about binding spells before, but this didn't feel anything like that. Those were just supposed to prevent people from using a certain object, or opening a particular lock. This felt like the sword was my third arm, and I couldn't leave it behind. I wondered what else the mages could do, and what would be the consequences of giving mages too much money? I couldn't get that fable out of my head. You know that one.[5] Maybe there was a reason nobody had funded the arcane arts this much before. Yeah,[6] I thought that even at the time.

I was coming up to the foothills. The map gave details for how to find the cave, but I didn't need them. I could smell the dragon.

Please understand I had never been this close to a dragon in my life. People saw them everywhere, but I'd been everywhere, and I'd never seen one, so I began to doubt they even existed. As soon as that smell hit my nose, I knew it couldn't have been anything else. Another clue: no animals anywhere. I followed my nose up the hillside.

---

5 *The story of the Witch Who Cursed the Baker, about a witch who attempts to curse a baker with bread that never rises only for the spell to backfire and open a gateway to the netherworld, into which she is pulled.*

6 The original sources use *Yow*, the precursor to the modern interjection.

How to describe it? A little like fish, but not the bad stench of rotting fish, or fish sitting at market. Smelled like a good meal at a tavern where they just barely cook the fish. I've been to some places where they don't cook it at all; they just cut the meat up and serve it with vegetables. That's the kind of smell it was, but much stronger. A bit like how you can tell a cow from a fox. Neither smell is bad. Just distinct.

I followed that up past the point where the grass ended. Thankfully it wasn't so high up I had to trudge through snow. I stopped about a hundred yards below it and decided to rest. I hoped the dragon would come out and I could escape back into the trees, but then I wondered. If I could smell the dragon like this, could it smell me? I'd be the only creature in a mile. It would be easy to find me even among the trees.

I knew nothing about dragons. Absolutely nothing, and I hadn't thought to ask. Did anyone know about dragons? I'd heard some wild stories over the years. Some man in a tavern said he saw one breathing ice and freezing a lake. A woman in another town said she saw one swallowing the sun. A dragon ate an entire herd of sheep. A dragon made a sinkhole in one farmer's field, and an elderly man told me he saw a dragon touch the ground and evaporate into a spirit that washed over the town, and not long after that, nine children fell dead.

I had no idea what to expect.

Poke and run.[7]

I built a small fire under a cliff, not sure if I hoped the dragon would smell it or not. I promised to strike as soon as I felt rested. I wanted to be ready to run for hours if I needed to. I amused myself pondering the idea that the dragon wouldn't feel a prick from something as small as sword no matter how big and sharp this was.

____

7 *Should be the title of this man's story.*

The sword grew to as long as a house's roof beam. The blade became so sharp I heard the air being cut as I waved it. It should have been heavy, but it was as light as paper in my grip. I tested it on the cliff face, and it sliced the rock clean. The impact had as much force as a weapon that weighed a hundred pounds.

The whole time, I didn't only feel that I held the sword. The sword also had a grip on me.

Then I had an idea. The sword could become any weapon I imagined, so I wondered if it could be used for defense, too. I experimented with making it change into a shield. Then I imagined it could become a shield that hid my presence. A dome that projected forest surroundings and hid my scent, too.

The sword seemed to have trouble with this one. It opened like the top of a fountain and poured down and around me. I still held the hilt, but the sword had now become a curtain surrounding me. I couldn't tell if it hid my scent, or if anyone could see me through it.

I tried walking, but the weapon couldn't hold its shape. It retracted back into the sword I had always wanted. It seemed to be its normal shape. Required no effort to hold it like that. Everything else I had to concentrate and will it to stay. I had just found a limit to what it could do. The mages hadn't mentioned limits, and now that my eyes were watering from all the dragon scent in the air, I felt a pang of worry.

I tried changing it into other objects. Bottles. Food. A mirror. A book. The sword could mimic the forms of these, but not always the functions I had in mind. The book did not open and had no individual pages. The bottles couldn't be opened. The food was solid. The mirror worked, though.

Apparently I couldn't make it become anything too specific, and I couldn't give it any other enchantments, so no changing it into a poison-tipped sword that would kill a dragon with a single stab.

I spent another few hours trying to make the sword become a pillow. I eventually made it soft enough to be comfortable but firm enough to hold my neck straight. I felt proud of myself for figuring out how to manipulate it.

At dawn, I found the fire cold, and the sword underneath me. It had collapsed back into its normal shape in my sleep.

I left everything that could make noise under the cliff and began the climb up the steep slope. That smell... By the time I got to the mouth of the cave, I could practically see the scent flowing like water on the ground. I hadn't heard anyone describe the smell of a dragon this way, so strong it became a mist on the ground. I had to hold my breath on the way inside.

I held the sword in front of me as I crept. It began to give off a faint glow. Glad it could do that. It meant I wouldn't have to make a torch.

I had time to notice the entrance was only large enough for a man, so how did the dragon get in? I figured there must be another entrance somewhere. It seemed a bit strange to me that there should be more than one way into this cave, but that wasn't really on my mind. Breathing was difficult enough, and trying to walk without making noise took a lot of effort.

The passage narrowed so much I had to squeeze through sideways, and it went on and on. I didn't realize it at the time, but later I went back and measured it. It's seventy yards deep, twisting and turning back and forth. If not for that smell and the mages telling me something was on the other end, I never would have risked such a tight squeeze for that long.

The cavern opened up, and there it was, fast asleep. It would easily fill the town square, but the cavern could have held five creatures its size.

It was blue. All the times I'd heard of dragons, nobody ever described one with blue scales. Black horns, red claws. Four legs. Wings sprouting from its shoulders. Its scales had different shades of blue all over. I remember pausing and staring at it for a moment. Blue patterns hidden inside of blue patterns. Blue highlights over the fingers. Darker blue stripes shimmering on the legs. I thought it was pretty.

I felt bad for what I had to do. I hated it when people woke me out of a sound sleep. I crept closer, parting the mist made of dragon scent with my ankles. I decided to go for the tail, hoping it wouldn't feel pain as bad as if I stabbed it in the face. Also I'd have more time to hide if I was farther away from its teeth. I walked down its flank so slowly I think I made the sword impatient. I could feel it pulling me onward. I had a feeling it wanted to get this over with as well. I passed the foreleg. The stomach. I could hear its heart beating, and its breath sounded like a storm. I came to one of the claws on a hind leg. Its claw was as long as me, and the paw, or hand, was half as tall as I was.

I looked the other way and noticed the cave walls were reflective. I could see myself creeping in front of the dragon's thigh. I would later realize the whole cave was made of obsidian, and I saw the dragon's reflection behind mine. Some facets were clearer than others, and some were so distorted I couldn't even make out my beard. This would have been a nice place to explore if not for the dragon sleeping in it.

I followed the tail as it tapered to the tip, and then paused again and just looked down its length. My first time seeing a dragon, and all I could think about was going back to that tavern and telling people the tale of the dragon I found in a cave. It wasn't doing anything. Just sleeping. What a boring story. I'd have to add that it was lying on a gigantic pile of shoes and dead babies so people would pay attention.[8]

It could swallow me whole and not even have to chew. I had a hard time believing it even existed. How could I not have seen one before? Why hadn't they burned the whole world by now? And why did mages need me to test a weapon on one? What was there to test?

Well, time to earn my fee.

While I wasn't looking, the sword had changed into a terrifying device of torture and slaughter. Serrated blade, multiple prongs coming out of the shaft like ice crystals. The sword had changed to a blue color, patterns inside of patterns, matching the scales of its target. Looking back on it, I think I was struck by those scales and I must have wanted my ideal sword to be that beautiful mix of colors, too.

I lunged. The sword slid through the scales vanished into its tail all the way up to the hilt, and for a brief instant, I believed the dragon wouldn't even feel it.

It gasped and raised its head. I wasn't taking any chances. I pulled back. The sword had lost its serrated edges and prongs, so it slipped out easily. Blood followed. I had planned to tell the mages that dragon blood was dark as wine and smelled about the same.

I ran to the cave wall, hoping it wouldn't see me. The floor trembled, and a five-clawed hand slammed down in front of me. I held my arms out to keep from falling as the ground shook, hoping nothing fell from the ceiling and crushed me.

I turned, and all I could see was a dragon's mouth. I only stood as tall as its shin, and the muzzle was the same

---

8 *He laughed at length at this point, giving us a moment to rest.*

size as me. It roared, and I held the sword out. It had already reshaped itself into a shield, and just in time; the cave lit up in flames. The fire flicked around the shield, but I still broke into a sweat. The dragon must have roasted me for a solid minute before it took a breath. The shield remained unscathed. I turned to the dragon's hand, raising the shield as it became a serrated nightmare blade again, but longer, thicker, bigger—far larger than I would have been able to wield naturally.

I chopped. The blade slid into the dragon's hand. The monster roared, lighting up the cave again in flames. It moved its hand out of the way, leaving a trail of thick blood behind, which is what I wanted. I righted myself as the sword shrank to knife-size and ran under the bleeding hand. It roared and stomped after me. I found the cave entrance and dashed for it.

The cave floor shook, and the dragon's tail crashed in front of me and curled inward. I slid to a stop and turned around. The dragon had surrounded me with its body, and now I stared at its teeth. I held the sword ready. In a couple seconds, the sword grew into a double-sided ax emitting light bright enough to rival the sun. I aimed the beam at the dragon's face, crossing an eye once. Twice. The dragon winced and raised a hand over me.

From the corner of my eye, I noticed its tail curling inward. Just as I thought. The hand was a distraction. It was going to whip me first and then claw me. I aimed my weapon at the approaching wall of blue flesh. The sword grew a point at the tip along the path of light it emitted, and the tail smacked into it.

The blade expanded in girth, and it grew spikes. The dragon roared and flicked its tail backwards. The blade slid off it, and I hopped backwards just as the hand crashed down where I had been. I swung again. The ax pierced its forearm. Still roaring, the dragon ran in a circle around me, creating a moving wall of blue scales. I turned with it, keeping its eyes in sight and the weapon between us.

It had green eyes. Slitted.

It didn't attack. I waited eagerly for it to make a move as I looked for an opening.

I noticed its wings rising, and as soon as I saw it, it flapped them in my direction. The force blew me backwards a few steps, and the sword became a shield again. I held it up, and it blocked the wind so I stayed on my feet.

An arm and the tail moved—it wanted to attack from three sides, and I wished the sword were long enough to reach the dragon's face. The shield melted before me and stretched out. I braced myself, but the dragon noticed and crouched under the reaching blade. I stopped it from growing just before it hit the cave wall, and then willed it to come back.

It took about four seconds before I noticed it retracting. The weapon could do everything I needed in a fight, but it didn't change forms quickly, and stupid me, I had just extended the weapon too far for me to use.

The dragon reached up with one hand and pushed the blade down to the ground. I tried to pull it out, but it hadn't shrunk far enough yet. The dragon turned and glared at me, and then it jumped on top of the blade. All four feet.

The blade bent, and then snapped in half.

Something inside me snapped, too. My heart. My bones. I saw the weapon evaporate. My hands evaporated with it. The dragon looked just as surprised as it fell to the ground.

You need a break? Sure, good place to pause. The good stuff is coming up right after this, so I hope you're ready.

SESSION 2

Everyone ready? Had some water, a bite to eat, went to the back?[9] Good, because here's where it starts to get interesting,[10] so get comfortable.

I didn't black out. The world started spinning. I was spinning around the cave. My vision became bands of clouds, and I saw the dragon in the cave from a different angle in each one, some swirling to the left, others to the right, some views crisscrossing.

The blue dragon wandered the cave, licking its blood off the floor and sniffing everywhere, probably to make sure no one else was here. It seemed to be moving many times faster than normal. When it was satisfied, it doubled over and began licking its wounds. Then I saw it lying down, apparently sleeping. It didn't move for a long time. When it stretched out and rolled over, the different bands in my vision came together, and I was lying on the dirt.

---

9 That is, to the restroom.

10 In 1166, King Nitae III of Kentor ordered the "unsuitable" passages rewritten to match the sensibilities of his upbringing, creating the custom of encoding physical intimacy into elaborate polite conversation within stories and songs, which in turn became custom among the aristocracy, which then became custom among the general population throughout multiple kingdoms. Scholars have reconstructed the Sessions from 6 original sources, and from dozens of fragments of salvaged copies that escaped the organized burning campaigns.

I was facing the cave wall about ten yards away, and I saw myself as I raised my head. As a human,[11] I hadn't been able to see in this dark cave, but now it looked as bright as midday, and a dragon's face was staring back at me. This dragon had green scales, white horns, and white claws. I jumped to my feet and confirmed I had four of them. I stumbled around for a moment before I figured out how to stand on four legs. I turned and looked at the blue dragon. It was still lying on its side, half-asleep. We were about the same size now, and being eye level with a dragon was enough to scare me shitless.

I opened my mouth and tried to speak, but only grunts and rumbles came out. I must have learned how to move on four feet quickly, because I was turning around, looking at myself from as many angles as I could on the walls.

Remember that rope I mentioned earlier, the one the mages tied me to the weapon with? I felt it again, and it led me straight to the blue dragon. I carefully put one foot in front of the other and walked in its direction.

I made it about four steps toward the blue dragon and then something jerked me to a stop. A wave moved through my body. It started between my hind legs and ran through me. I looked down at my hands, and my fingers filled out and lengthened. The wave rose up my neck and down my face, and I saw my new muzzle extend about half a yard. My eye level had also risen.

Another wave hit me, this one starting in my chest, and I looked down. My chest muscles were filling out. My forelegs were also getting thicker, scales falling into crevices as the individual muscles pushed up through them. In a moment, I couldn't see my feet over my chest. I felt waves

---

[11] Originally, *man*. The word *human* did not exist colloquially then, though some manuscripts use it, likely a transcription change during the fifteenth century.

hitting my neck and moving through my legs. I turned my head to see what was happening.

The view of myself in the cave wall was split between two facets, but it was enough to help me understand what was going on. My dragon body was bulking out, but it was happening in waves that began at my crotch and washed over the rest of me. This wave hit me, and my skin stretched taut, and now cords of muscle ran underneath. My stomach had receded, and all that was left were rippling abdominals. Maybe twenty of them in sight.

My chest stuck so far in front of me it looked comical. My legs were rock solid. I tested one of them, lifting it off the ground, and the muscles contracted. They were packed so tight together the leg nearly doubled in thickness just using my muscles like this. My scales were so tight I saw every twitch of every fiber underneath them.

The forelegs impressed me most. I guess I still saw myself as a human, so the biceps caught my eye. I turned my hand over, clenched my fist and gave it a flex. It wasn't just one muscle; it was four, and as I moved them, they all swelled up beyond the size of my head, pushing one another thicker and taller. The detail looked amazing.

As I looked at it, it grew again. The other one stretched and filled out. My neck rose another yard up, and I had to adjust my stance as the wave hit the rest of me. In the cave walls, I saw everything pushing outward, and my height rising at the same time. Three more waves hit me like this, and I was now twice the height of the blue dragon, and easily thrice as bulky.

The other dragon had rolled to his back. His eyes were closed. He was half-asleep. Oh yes, now I knew it was a he because he was out of his slit, on full display.

I glanced at myself in the cave wall again. I'd seen hundreds of drawings and images of dragons before, but none of them looked like this. I pushed off the ground and rose to my hind legs. I was still trying to frame myself in human terms, so I needed to stand like a human to understand what I was looking at. Not easy to do on backwards legs, but I managed to look myself over in a posture I understood.

My arms were so thick I couldn't keep them at my sides. My chest muscles were larger than my head, and I couldn't see my toes when I looked down—all I saw was my chest. I counted at least thirty abdominal muscles along my stomach. Even my long neck had rippling definition. I was so bulky I wondered if I could move.

My legs struggled to hold me up, and then I dropped to all fours again. I made a crashing sound that echoed in the cave. Now the blue dragon opened his eyes and looked over at me. He barely breathed for two whole minutes as I stood there, and he just gazed. I took a step toward him, lowering my neck down to his eye level. My chest muscles pushed against each other. My biceps puckered my chest. My thighs rubbed together. I even felt muscles in my back rubbing against one another. But I could move. I tried to speak, but again just grumbling sounds came out.

Remember that uncooked fish smell I mentioned earlier? I caught it again, but now it had a different effect on me. Now it went straight from my nose to my groin. I didn't have nuts anymore, but the tingling feeling felt the same. I went straight to his cock. It didn't smell like fish anymore. Now that smell... Well, I guess human languages have no words for it. Try to imagine perfume that smells so good it makes you hard, so you want to keep breathing it, and finally you just have to fuck something.

I kept sniffing it. Then I licked it. It was about as long as my new muzzle and had spines and ridges, all of them soft and fleshy. In the back of my head, I knew what I was doing, but at the same time I couldn't get enough of that smell.

Bluey just lay there, letting me inspect him. He later told me as far as he knew, I had just arrived. Some muscular dragon dropped in and began lapping up the scent coming from his slit. God, it tasted good. I actually felt my belly filling up just licking it. Just thinking about it makes me hard. Sorry.

It was going straight to my groin. I felt something hot slipping out from between my legs. I pulled away from B's crotch and checked myself. My new dick looked similar to his. Long, tapered, ropelike, fleshy barbs and prongs lining the tip. My sense of scale was completely distorted by now, but the thing was as long as my arm and about half as thick. Dripping in clear fluid. Forgot to mention that. The slit between my legs was dripping so much I had made a little lake underneath me.

A wave hit me.

My dick expanded in a wave from my crotch down to the tip. Now it was as thick as my over-muscled foreleg.

I turned and looked at my blue observer. He was rubbing himself as he craned his neck to see. His fingers were playing with his fleshy barbs.

I looked over at the wall. My dick now reached my chest, and it was almost as thick as my torso. I turned down, and it peeked between my chest muscles. I felt it underneath me, slithering like a snake, slick and throbbing.

Little B was still on his back, rubbing himself faster, completely oblivious to these waves moving through me. I wanted to do something about that, but my expanding dick distracted me too much. The barbs were rubbing against my stomach, and the thing was hot.

My legs lifted off the ground. I looked at the wall, and sure enough I was lying on my dick, claws dangling just over the dirt.

Waves hit me. My legs stretched and thickened, and I could stand again, but now it looked like even my dick had muscles. As the waves traveled through me, I rose higher, my shoulders became thicker, and my chest obscured more of my downward vision.

Then I smelled something. Next thing I knew, I was down on the ground licking the blue dragon's seed. He made a lot of it, and it filled me up. I kept my mouth over his dick as he finished for what must have been five minutes, swallowing everything.

I don't remember exactly what happened next. The next thing I can remember I was back down to his eye level, dick hidden, a normal green dragon again. I still had more muscle on me than should have been possible. Still couldn't see my feet under my chest. After I had turned around a couple times, examining myself from all angles, I heard footsteps approaching. The blue dragon was walking up to me. I faced him.

He stood nose to nose with me, scenting me. Then he rubbed snouts. I was so delirious, still trying to get a grip on what was happening I couldn't even remember my name, or how I got there, so I rubbed him back. He smelled so good my nose led me down to his crotch and I licked his slit again. That's the right word for it, yes? Thanks.[12]

He let me do that for a minute, and then he circled me, sniffing and poking me with his snout. I stood in place, not sure what to do. I felt exhausted and full, as if I'd had a full

____

[12] Not every scribe rendered these asides. This edition seeks to include as much of the original text from as many sources as possible. Only passages verified by handwriting or historical analysis as authentic and original have been included.

side of lamb at a tavern, and this dragon's scent was the mug of cider.

I hung my head and panted I was so tired. He examined me and scented me up and down. I felt a hand on my thigh, and I turned to look at him. He was feeling the muscles, testing them, as if he couldn't believe they were solid. They gave to his touch, and when I moved one, it bulged out and became like a tree trunk. His hand wandered to my flank, and being touched reassured me I was still real. Once in a while he paused and looked at me, as if expecting me to vanish or attack or something. I didn't feel real until now. His fingers on my scales told me I had skin. His hands exploring the lines between the muscles made me feel like a living creature. I licked his snout this time when he hesitated, and he continued exploring me. The contact felt amazing, and his scent made me feel like I was lying in a field on a beautiful summer afternoon.

He felt my foreleg up. I held my arm out and flexed the muscles for him, and he marveled how he couldn't get his hands around my arm. He seemed to like feeling my chest muscles, and also my shoulders. When he felt my neck, I moved with his hands, hoping to show him I liked this, too, and I really did. Being touched helped me settle into this new skin.

Finally he stood in front of me again, nuzzling me. I nosed him back. For the first time I noticed the wounds I had inflicted on him earlier had healed, as if I had never stabbed him with the sword. I didn't smell blood anywhere. All I could smell was whatever was coming out of his slit.

He seemed to have calmed down by now. The fog of scent had cleared up, and no more waves hit me. I felt completely exhausted. I was huge, but I felt so small now compared to a few minutes ago.

The big blue dragon was grunting at me and huffing through his nose. Then he waited, as if expecting something. I looked at him, then looked at my arms again. No waves. Nothing happened.

The dragon turned halfway around and gestured upward. I looked up and noticed the reflective walls extended so far I couldn't see where they ended. A large hole in the wall yawned a couple hundred yards up, and the blue dragon had just spread his wings. I looked back at my wings. I didn't know how to move them, so I had forgotten about them.

The blue dragon flapped a few times and rose into the air with such ease and grace I thought it deserved a poem or something. He hovered in place and looked down at me. I didn't know what I should do, so I started moving muscles in my back.

What? Well, it's interesting to me! You'd dwell on it, too, if you woke up one day walking on four legs and had wings.

Anyway, I found the muscles that made my wings move and tested them. Just as I was starting to wonder if my wings were large enough to lift me off, a wave hit me, and my wings stretched longer and bulked out. I looked back at them, and finally they looked like enough to raise me off the ground, and on one flap, I did.[13]

I followed him through a tunnel, which was also lined in slippery obsidian. I tried to think back on any descriptions I'd heard of these mountains, but I couldn't remember anyone mentioning a cave system covered in glass. I watched myself walk. I could see the muscles under my scales. Every twitch, every pucker, every stretch. Just walking normally like this made them double in thickness. I was

---

13 No surviving manuscript contains the flight up to the cave. It is presumed the scribes considered learning to fly an unimportant tangent and stopped writing.

intimidated by the reflections I saw. As a hired sword, if I had seen a dragon like this anywhere, I would have given my employer their money back and fled to the next kingdom. Maybe two kingdoms and across the sea, just to be safe.

When we got outside, I was surprised to see trees and grass. Also surprising: I didn't have to wait for my eyes to adjust. The light seemed just the same as the inside of the cave.

I saw a plateau of trees of grass tucked between a cluster of mountain peaks. Weird trees. Weird grass. The trees themselves had no leaves; the bark was green, and the branches twisted and curved in and around each other. The grass also grew in curls. The people in this kingdom had never mentioned a place like this, so I guessed no human had ever seen it before. My blue companion huffed and made throaty growls as he took to the air. I flapped my over-muscled wings and followed him.

As I flew over this place, I looked out over the mountain ranges. My vision was so good I could see individual trees on top of peaks that were miles away. They looked so vivid even from this distance. I could make out animals. Strange animals that I knew didn't live among men. The blue dragon banked and dove. I didn't follow but hovered in midair. From here, I watched him land. He killed a gryphon. I had only heard of these animals before; never in my life did I think I would ever see one. I dismissed them as tavern stories, just like dragons, but the blue dragon had just taken one out with no fight.

He stood over the kill and looked up at me. He then hopped up on his hind legs a couple times like an excited puppy. I didn't know how to dive, so I flapped lighter and descended to the ground, touching down on two feet and then dropping to all fours. I walked up to him. Walking felt weird. Arms always colliding with my chest, thighs scraping together, shoulder muscles pushing against my neck.

The dragon ripped the body open and held out a piece of meat for me. I wasn't hungry, but it felt wrong to refuse, so I opened my mouth and took it.

The meat fell through my jaw and splattered on the ground.

The blue dragon recoiled, slinking lower, glancing between me and the meat.

I turned to him, then the meat, then the sky, then the curly trees and grass. I looked all around me.

Now I recognized where I was. I had been in places like this before. Mages and court wizards sent people like me to these areas from time to time. Places where magical plants grew, magical objects were hidden, and enchanted creatures lived. Dangerous places. They always looked shadowy and lethal. The leafless trees looked like bones sticking up from the ground in agony. The grass was thorny and seemed to move when you weren't watching.

The Netherworld. Mages and alchemists spoke of it often, always in hushed tones. They warned me to be careful when they sent me to one of those places that kind of bled into the Netherworld, that things didn't behave normally, that plants and animals were strange and if I went too far in, I would never return. I was in one of those places right now. At some point, I had crossed over into the Netherworld itself, and it looked like a child's drawing of springtime to me now.

It finally hit me. I was not human anymore; I was now one of those dangerous creatures that lived in the Netherworld, and now I just discovered I couldn't eat.

I stumbled around on my four legs, trying to make noise, trying to shout for help. Try to imagine remembering words but being unable to use them. To try again and again but nothing works the way you think it should.

I forgot how to fly, so I galloped away. I deliberately ran into trees and knocked them down. Some of the trees reached out for me and entangled me, but I easily broke free and pushed them aside. If I had come to this place as a human, I would have been terrified of these trees, but now they fell before me.

Some clumps of grass reached out to me and attached themselves to my feet. I felt little teeth trying to bore holes in my scales, no doubt to suck my blood or soul or something, but they couldn't break through. I kept running, trying to speak, trying to scream for help.

I was starting to run out of breath, and I felt a rope tightening around my throat. I felt as if I had left something behind. Something important. I fought the feeling and kept running, hoping if I ran far enough I'd end up back in the land of men.

Air was all around me, but I couldn't breathe it.

The rope seemed to be pulling me backwards. I collapsed to my stomach as I gasped and gagged. The grass now suckled on my belly and thighs, searching for an opening. A tubular branch of one tree had wrapped around my foot, but I was too heavy for it to pull.

Moments later, the blue dragon's scent hit my nose, and suddenly I had air. The rope slackened. I felt like a leg that had just been reunited with the body. I stopped trying to scream and just breathed. Not air. Scent. B's scent. It didn't go straight to my groin this time.

I felt him standing over me, nuzzling me, making low growls that I hoped were noises of concern and compassion. He started to rub his head against mine, and then he lay next to me. I couldn't run anymore. I just lay there and breathed. His scent was apparently my air now.

I let that thought ferment in my mind for a while.

His touch did feel reassuring, and eventually I started to rub my head against his.

The dragon made some other sounds. Grunts and whines and whistles, and he kept rubbing his muzzle against mine. I raised my head off the ground, separating myself from a couple hundred strands of grass trying to chew on me, and looked at him. He began to whimper. All the stories I'd ever heard about dragons, nobody had ever described a dragon whimpering. It sounded so strange I forgot about the trees and grass trying to pull me apart. I forgot I wasn't human. I reached up and petted his head like a dog.

I had never touched a lizard before. The only lizards I'd ever been around were snakes I'd killed in the forest. His scales felt... nice. Like the quilt my grandmother made that kept me warm as I rode in the back of my father's cart as a boy.

Whimpering, he opened his mouth and coughed fire on my face.

It hit me so fast I didn't even react. I knew I had been hit by fire—the same stuff that almost melted me an hour ago, but now I didn't even feel it. He stared at me as I had my hand between his horns. He whimpered again.

After blinking a few times, I opened my mouth and tried to cough onto him, but nothing happened. He sniffed the inside of my mouth, standing up after a moment. Whatever he smelled in there must have been interesting. I wanted to ask him so many questions, and at the same time I still wanted to run for the hills.

Nuzzling my snout, he lifted a foreleg and bumped me on the side. I took the hint and rolled over. My wings tucked tight against my sides without me telling them to, and I lay sprawled out like a dog.

The blue dragon backed up and stood by my tail, looking up my body. He sniffed my thighs and my crotch. Finally I had a chance to look at my underside, and no, I had no balls or dick anymore. Just a slit between my legs, and he was burying his blue muzzle in it. It felt good, in a way. He kept pausing and looking at me, and I wasn't sure why at the time. It was weird, but I didn't want him to stop either, so I spread my legs farther apart. He seemed to take that as a sign to continue, and now I felt a tongue in there.

The noises I made...[14]

Please understand, this was not my first time with a man. I'd already broken a few laws of nature in my life, and when you're on a mission in the middle of nowhere, and your only company for weeks is another man, and both of you are in the mood, and nobody is watching, and there's a very real chance you will die tomorrow, both of you just say fuck it and start playing around. I guess I had been looking forward to those employers who needed me to go to some distant fortress off the beaten path, and they wanted to send someone else with me. That's when it was fun. When you're alone with someone, and you just throw caution out the window and show him your dick. Odds are he'll recognize you're out alone and nobody else will ever know, so why not try it? I've had more than one person ask to come with me a second or third time over my life. Never been with the same person more than three times[15] though.

So, yes, I wasn't all that surprised by this. When my dick slipped out and the blue muzzle started licking it up, it felt just like those jobs. It didn't seem unusual until I noticed my dick changing shape. A wave moved up my crotch, and my cock grew. It had been about as long as his muzzle

---

14 *He made those noises. Even to human ears, they sounded like bedroom noises.*

15 Some manuscripts render this as *thrice*. The language was still in transition regarding the use of this word in the year 893, when M told his story.

and maybe as thick as a couple of my new fingers—hard to remember, my sense of scale was all messed up then—and it had soft barbs around the tip. Now it grew more of those fleshy ridges all up and down, and it doubled in size.

So now I was staring at a dick as thick as my bulging arm and with so many barbs and ridges I couldn't count them.

Another wave rushed up, and it stretched another yard. The dragon was now looking up at it as he ran his tongue from the base midway to the tip.

A wave hit me. I moaned, and it lengthened and swelled again, the ridges becoming deeper, the barbs sticking out more. The thing towered over me like a steeple, and B was now on his hind legs, feeling it all around, teasing the barbs. Everything he did went straight to my groin, and I humped the air a few times. He wrapped his arms around it and looked down at me, making more of those concerned noises. I panted and bucked my hips a couple times, brushing him with a few ridges.

That feeling began in my crotch again and spread out to the rest of my body. My thighs thickened, my tail shot out, pushing a few trees aside. My whole upper body swelled. When the feeling passed, I had more abdominal muscles. Lots of them all around my stomach, and I had to lean up to see them over my chest. My chest had swollen, and a quick glance at my arms revealed biceps and forearms out of proportion again.

I looked back up at him. He was still on his hind legs, hugging my dick, and now he was out of his slit again.

The wind blew his scent over me, and it was like being in that one place you always retreated to as a child, where nothing could touch you. I rose from the hips and met him snout to snout. I bumped him. He bumped me back, and then I expanded again. I grew another yard taller. I reached up and felt my neck, and sure enough the rippling muscles had deepened. My chest had doubled in thickness, and the abdominal muscles also stood out more. I tested my arms. The bicep peaked halfway up my forearm, and when I relaxed the muscle, it barely fell.

The dragon was still hugging my cock, looking me over from crotch to muzzle. He licked his lips a few times, and I leaned down and licked B on his muzzle. I at least wanted him to know this felt good. Every time a wave hit me was like blowing a load in the woods, knowing another man had made it happen, and nobody but us would ever know.

I panted and moaned as another wave swelled up in my groin, and my neck rose another half yard above the dragon's. My dick grew with it, now a pillar, and the dragon couldn't get his arms around it. I checked my arm, and the bicep now peaked halfway up my forearm without flexing it. I made a muscle, and the forearm collided with it, making a solid wall.

My neck rose again, and the shock sent me to my back, and I lay sprawled out as everything swelled from my crotch outward.

The blue dragon dropped from my dick and lay on my chest. His muzzle fit perfectly between my pectorals, and he looked at me, both hands groping them. They were hard, but they still moved with his touch. He was feeling my abs with one of his feet, and his scent filled my head so much nothing else existed. I couldn't see beyond him. No sky. No land. No light. In my mind, he was the only thing that existed.

I wrapped my arms around him and held him close. Immediately, I grew again, and my muscles squeezed him tighter between them. My cock was still pointing straight up, slick and shiny and pulsing, the ridges and barbs moving in time.

He was panting and moaning, and I felt his hips bucking and his own ridges rubbing against my stomach.

I tried to smile, but my face didn't do that anymore, so I flexed my arms and chest.

They swelled again, practically imprisoning him between my pecs and biceps.

This was fun in a way, and now I knew exactly what he wanted. Holding him tight against me, I rolled over and pinned him to the ground under one of my forefeet. If I was right about this, he would do the rest. All I had to do was go where he led me.

I pinned him beneath one of my feet and stood over him, making sure he could see nothing but my chest and stomach. My dick was so big I could see the tip poking out between my legs. He reached up with all four legs like a cat and held my hand. I looked down at him and growled.

As I expected, my groin tingled, and everything swelled. My chest expanded, my biceps bulked out so far they collided with my forearms even without flexing them; my dick slid even further past my chest. My head had risen a yard up, and I had to adjust my stance to keep looking at him. Whoever this dragon was, he liked his men big, and he liked to be at their mercy. I could do that. I'd done it before to human men when that was what they wanted, and I usually got paired with younger, less experienced mercenaries, so they liked being under me. Some of the older mercenaries I'd been with liked it that way, too. Now that I was in familiar territory, I felt far more comfortable.

I grew again, but this time I noticed my claws grew more than the rest of me. The tingling had spread to the horns on my head, and I figured they must have extended as well.

And then a new feeling hit me. My shoulders tingled in a way they never had before. I looked over and saw spines coming out of them. No blood. The scales just parted to make room. They grew curved and long. Dozens of them. All up and down my arms.

I pushed him harder into the ground, rubbing him a little. My reward was these new spines growing even bigger as the muscles swelled. I adjusted my stance, making sure to stand so my chest muscles pushed against each other. He liked that; my abs tightened and bulked, and that feeling flooded my chest, and the muscles grew again. The tingling spread to my arms, and they swelled again.

I found a new muscle, and my dick raised off the ground. I tried to laugh again as I raised my dick at the same time, swung it over him, and let it fall. I practically squished him under my cock, and he hugged it like a cat that had just caught a mouse. I couldn't see him anymore underneath it.

The tingling feeling began again, but it felt different. I could tell something big was about to happen because the sensation made me cringe. My height rose twenty yards in a single breath, and the rest of me also expanded about that much, too. Thighs became thick enough to touch even when standing with my legs apart. Chest and biceps rubbed against each other no matter how I stood. My dick was at least twice as long as my body and pulsing enough to make the barbs and ridges dance.

I had just blown a load all over the forest. The trees in front of me had no idea what to do, and they were swinging around in a panic, trying to shake the stringy mess away.

I flexed my stomach muscles and lifted my dick. B was there, covered in my slick and his semen. As soon as I saw it I bent down and lapped it up. My head was the size of his whole body now. Difficult to believe when I first walked into that cave that he could have swallowed me whole.

I tried to make my mouth move like a human, forced my throat to make human sounds so I could tell him you are one perverted son of a bitch, but that was fun.

I only grunted at him as he drank in the sight of me standing over him. I wish I could have seen myself. He had made me so huge I probably could have moved a mountain.

I stepped away from him, and he rolled to his feet and observed the damage I had inflicted. As he looked at the trees covered in cum and flailing about, he turned to me and breathed fire all over my face. It didn't hurt me at all, and I learned my first lesson of dragon behavior: dragons laugh by blowing fire on each other. My blue companion was drenching me in flames, and I tried to return it. No fire came out of my mouth, so I did my best to laugh like a human.

It must have taken me five whole minutes to come back down, and I watched myself the whole time. The extra spines slipped back into my skin as if they had never been there. My dick became disappointingly normal and shrank back between my legs. I stopped shrinking at about a yard taller than my blue partner. My muscles did not shrink all the way. My chest still collided with my arms, my thighs were still thick enough to meet when standing, my neck still had bulgy cords running up and down it. I looked under myself, and I had about twenty abdominal muscles lining my midsection.

I turned to B. He made affectionate sounds at me and licked my muzzle. I bumped him back. I tried to imagine this from his point of view. Did he know I used to be a thinking human being? Had he made that connection? Was I the man of his dreams? I hoped so. That was the best sex I'd ever had, and I hadn't even put my dick into anything yet.

All right, I tried to say. I can't eat normal food, but I can lick your jizz. I don't breathe air anymore. I breathe your scent. This means... We're stuck together. I could think of worse places to be. I felt relieved to become whatever this dragon desired.

He seemed to react to my random grunts trying to be words. He felt my arm, concentrating on the tricep as I stood there. He couldn't wrap his hands around my arm, and this fascinated him. I looked out over the land. It didn't seem so intimidating anymore, especially knowing I had a guide.

Night began to fall, but the only way I could tell was that the sun was disappearing. The level of light did not seem to vary for me, and I wondered if dragons even needed light to see. I didn't feel tired, and B didn't either. He flapped his wings and took to the air. My wings were muscular enough to lift two of me, I figured.

The valley was much bigger than I had realized. We followed the entire mountain chain. Or so I thought at first. I looked at things from a human perspective then, and we seemed to be flying above a valley between two sets of mountains. Below me I saw all sorts of strange plants and animals, all of them mythical, some of them things I'd been hired to fetch at some point in the past.

I had no idea where we were. I saw no familiar features. Nothing to remind me of home.[16]

Oh, you need a break? Ah, I can smell some of you do. Well, go and take care of yourselves. I won't judge. In fact, you don't even have to leave. Jizz is the only thing I can eat, you know.

------

16 Only one surviving manuscript contains the following paragraphs at the end of Session 2. Handwriting analysis confirms they are authentic and not a later addition, the work of one diligent scribe, the last to receive any personal attention from M.

Yes, you. Keep rubbing. Keep thinking about giant, muscular dragons standing over you, about to crush you, but he doesn't because he wants you to live.

That's just what I needed. Yes, thank you. Anyone else? You next. I'll help. You ever have a dragon suck you off? You want to? I don't bite. Unless you want me to.

Don't finish without me. There's nine of you and only one of me.

I was hoping they'd pick people who really wanted to hear this story in all its detail. You don't mind if I grow in here, do you? B likes to make it happen at the most inappropriate moments. You should see us when we're with other dragons. He loves showing up all the bigger males, making sure they know I can be bigger than them at any time. It's a big deal among dragons, even more so than men. I end up fucking so many that way. It keeps peace among us. That's why sodomy is banned by the Church, you know. They know if men were free to fuck each other, there would be no war, and that means no profit for all the people who make weapons, which means the Church gets less tithe. Laugh if you want, but I've seen your world from the outside, and I'm here to tell you that's what's going on. It's the solution to all your problems. Just let the men fuck.

You taste good. Who's next?

You realize now I have all of your scents and I can find you again no matter where you are in the world? Dragons can do that. Did you know that? Oh, don't look so worried. Me and B are content with each other. Usually. I like humans. He doesn't, but he lets me indulge once in a while, so if I land in your town, you know there's only way to keep me from destroying it.

I'm kidding. I'm kidding. Learn when I'm laughing.

I suppose it's a good idea to call it a night. We meet again tomorrow.

SESSION 3

Hey, everyone's here. I knew you'd be back. All nine of you.

Yes, I knew where all of you were. I really can sense it. I can smell where you are no matter where you are in the world. All dragons can smell where their mates are at any time, and my body thinks anyone whose jizz I eat is my mate, so I have a lot of partners in my head. I think it's a gift.

So I left off at...?[17]

Thanks.[18] So now we were flying over this huge place. No more mountains. The weird trees had given way to something like a grassland. No grass though. I mean instead of trees and grass, I saw flowers, but they didn't have stems. Just a vast sea of purple and black flowers.

A building came up over the horizon. A temple made of stone. Now I've been in places like this before. All of them are ancient and crumbling. Most people are terrified to set foot in them. Monsters and evil magic and such. I never encountered anything like that in the ones I went to.

This place coming up looked like it had been built yesterday. A series of stone mesas rising to a peak. B turned and dove straight for it. We landed on the lowest tier, about six yards above the ground.

---

17 *We refreshed his memory, reminding him not to go out of sequence too much.*

18 *I'm here to get another blowjob from a dragon.*

Strange smells swirled around me, but I couldn't place any of them. My nose practically screamed at me all the time and I hadn't learned how to sort out all the different smells yet.

From the corner of my eye, I saw a woman. A human woman. I turned, but nothing was there except bare rock. Then I saw another person just on the edge of my vision. I turned my head, and I couldn't see him anymore.

B had just sat down, looking at the flat stone ground. I saw someone moving again, to my extreme right. This time I didn't turn, and now I knew people were here.

I watched B from the corner of my eye, and I caught glimpses of people kneeling before him, bowing to him. Maybe worshiping him.

I felt someone touch me, and I turned and looked, startled, not surprised when I saw nothing.

I noticed pedestals where flames would have been. They were empty here, but as I turned my head to the side I caught a glimpse of fires roaring in them.

Now I recognized this place. I had been here before, as a human. Ran a few messages and warnings of attack to and from this temple, home of the South Sect. My mind did a few tumbles because it was south of the kingdom of Harlu, a full three-month's journey away from Hirinda.

I could not comprehend traveling that far in so short a time.

When I had been there, the temple was in ruins, as they always were—vestiges of earlier times when magic was less understood, and various cults devoted their lives to taming these forces. Most ended up destroying themselves misusing a spell in one way or another. South Sect had been no different, but the people who lived there now claimed to feel the presence of magic stronger here than anywhere else.

I hadn't felt anything then, but now I saw them, and somehow they knew me and B were here. I turned in place, glimpsing lots of people gathering around me. That's when I remembered how big I was. How I must have looked to these people.

Someone bumped me, and this one felt solid. I turned to look. B was standing next to me, wings outstretched.

I felt a wave coming and braced myself just in time for my arms to double in thickness. Legs did the same thing. Chest puffed out so far I couldn't see my feet again.

I glimpsed people dropping to their knees. Faint whispers of chants drifted up from the stone.

B was flaming me on my arm, laughing, and then he turned away. He flapped his wings and took to the air.

I thought I might be too big to fly now, but my wings covered half the mesa. They lifted me without trouble.

The vast ocean of flowers yielded to a swamp filled with some sort of black goo. I noticed animals playing in it as if it were water. Animals I had no idea what to call. Later I would learn they were hippogryphs and sphinx and Baku. I saw pixies fluttering about as well.

A place like this could have easily been a wizard's hunting ground. In my head I tried to add up all the mystical ingredients at play down there: the sphinx blood, the hippogryph claws, the fairy wings.

The longer we flew over it, the less like a swamp it seemed. The black goo did not stick to anything. It seemed to be just the same as water, and the vegetation around it bloomed in brilliant pink flowers. Not really trees. It was as if parts of the black goo became solid and hung over the less solid parts, and fruit grew on these pieces. Once the fruit had been picked, the branch became liquid again and sank back into the rest of the mass.

Just then I noticed B flying beside me, no longer in the lead. Something about his posture told me he wanted to know if I wanted to go down there. I banked left, and this time he followed me all the way down. I chose a place where I saw people standing on top of the black goo.

As I touched down, I expected to sink. Other people were swimming, diving, so even though I saw people standing in this part, I wasn't prepared when I stayed on top. I stood there, bracing myself, not knowing what to do, and I could feel my thighs collide as they flexed. My chest puckered between my forelegs as they held me up, preparing me to jump.

The ground looked like liquid coal, but it shined when the light hit it right. I saw my reflection in it, and I looked like a nightmare creature. I had enormous horns crowning my head, each one coming to a point in front me, other horns lining my face and ringing my eyes. My shoulders had spikes coming out of them—didn't remember those, or when they appeared.

And of course, my pecs almost touched the ground they were so huge. The rest of me was just as bulky. Every time I moved, it was like watching ropes moving under a sail. My scales were still green, but the spikes were blood red, and branching away from those spikes were rivers of red. Blood vessels. They looked like a lava flow across my skin, and they snaked over and between my entire body.

Blood was flowing outside my body. My blood was glowing.

I looked at B, hoping I looked bewildered. He stood flank to flank with me, the same height but only a quarter of my mass.

A crowd was gathering.

Until my little blue dragon, I had never seen a mythical creature alive. That's what they were. Myths. Things people told stories about in taverns but few could actually claim to have seen. People who practiced the magical arts cared more about these creatures than anyone because their fur, or eyes, or blood, or bile, or something had magical properties. I had been sent to some strange places to retrieve magical herbs, and I had even retrieved some hair samples that some mage told me was yeti fur and paid me to go back and scavenge for more. I didn't fully believe her, but I took her money.

Now I saw a few yeti standing atop the lake of black slime, right next to a few kitsune, two-headed rabbits, snake-horses, unicorns, and dozens of other creatures I couldn't name. They were hard to read, but they seemed in awe of me.

B was making grunting and huffing noises. I stood still and listened. B suddenly roared, and then everyone turned to me.

Son of a bitch, I thought. He's showing me off.

A tiny wave moved through my throat, and I opened my mouth and let loose a roar that probably scared some horses in a few kingdoms.[19]

What? Oh, you didn't know that? Sound can travel between the magical realm and yours, just as sometimes animals get lost and wander between the realms. The barrier between this world and the Netherworld can weaken for no apparent reason, and that allows animals and plants to cross over once in a while. In some places the barrier is permanently weak, and that's the best way to find mystical objects. Half the rotting temples and shrines in the world are halfway in the magical realm, and that's why they're so dangerous, but I'll get to that later.

So I roared, making a wave in the goo, and all the solid branches collapsed in its wake. The goo seemed to shiver,

---

19 *The scribe from Exliland asked for clarification.*

and the people around us sank. Me and B remained on solid ground, and when I ran out of breath, I stood proud.

Their scents had changed. I didn't understand how at the time, but I still guessed they were awed. So was I. My crotch began tingling, and I slipped out of my slit. Another wave hit, and I felt it rubbing against my stomach, brushing me with barbs and ridges. I realized my chest and arms were too thick for them to see it, so I turned halfway around. I bared my teeth. I hoped it was a grin to them.

I watched my reflection in the goo as my cock went from as thick as my finger to as thick as my arm, and about as bulgy. The tip reached my chest, and I raised one foreleg so they could see better. Suddenly it doubled in size and became as thick as my whole torso, lifting my feet off the ground.

People were screaming and running away. A few others stood and stared.

One more wave, and the barbs and ridges emerged all at once, but this time the entire thing was covered in fleshy spines. Now the rest of the crowd ran away, some making noise that I hoped was laughter.

I turned to B, whose neck had curled back in surprise. I licked him and bobbed my neck, trying to mimic him when he breathed fire on me. I still couldn't do it. I hoped he understood I was trying to laugh with him.

I got the feeling people assumed dragons were animals. The people who claimed to have seen one all described them in animal terms, so what would happen if an animal had control of me? Would he comprehend it, and what would he do with someone that could assume any shape at will?

Apparently, all the mythical creatures were more than animals, and my blue dragon could talk to them. It had only been a day, and I'd already figured out how he laughed, so maybe I could learn his language.

B spread his wings and took off. I somehow lifted off with a dick the size of my whole body dangling beneath me. As we flew around the marsh, it hid inside my slit again. I don't know if it actually shrank; I didn't feel it this time.

He took me to a few other places. Strange caves, bizarre landscapes. One of the caves I recognized. I had been inside it just a few months ago to retrieve whatever I could from the fenrir[20] that had been spotted in the area.

As I expected, this cave seemed to be one of those places where the Netherworld—the realm I was in with B—kind of mixed with the human one. It had a border, where the cave became dim and everything seemed different. I confirmed that the human side looked dark and dangerous to me now.

B and I faced that border in one part of the cave. I could see it perfectly in one of the larger chambers. Ancient people had built a city here and had experimented with magic. No way to know what happened to them, but now parts of it had collapsed, all of it was in decay, people had scavenged everything of value long ago. You had to squeeze through a narrow passageway full of fallen boulders and rubble just to reach this part. Giant wolves lived here, and they seemed to avoid this divide. Only stupid humans who needed money dared cross the line from the human world to the Netherworld. I had, years ago. I risked my life for fenrir fur or urine or shit—mages wanted anything related to these mythical dogs. Their shit was magical. I laughed at it then and took their money. I wasn't laughing now.

---

20 Not *the* Fenrir of ancient stories. The giant wolves which inspired the story are named after him.

I looked at B. He was backing away, trying to encourage me to turn around. I turned back to the border. I had to know, so I set a hand on the other side.

Nothing happened, but I sure felt the difference. It felt like home. I took another step and slipped my head through. It felt like being underwater, all the colors and sounds muted, and then I caught a scent. I had been catching scents all day, but none of them made sense until *this* one.

I stepped the rest of the way in, and I scented this spot. I remembered it. Years ago, I had placed a hand on this broken pillar. The scent was still strong, and it was *my* scent. Somehow I recognized it.

B was on the other side of the veil, making whiny sounds and stamping his feet. I turned to him and made similar whining sounds, tapping a claw on the pillar. He didn't want to budge. I whined louder as I scented the spot and tapped my claw against it.

Gradually, B moved toward the barrier, skulking like a fox. He hesitated, and then ran through, straight to the pillar. I made room for him, and he scented my hand print—I could practically see it, as if my eyes sensed it now, too.

B looked at the pillar, then me, then scented the pillar, then scented me. I sat down on my haunches, chest muscles pushing my arms out, thighs so large they touched even in this position all the way down to the knees.

B touched the handprint on the wall, visible only in scent, and then reached out and touched me on the snout.

I nodded. I made cooing and whining sounds. I bounced my ass and wagged my tail. I did everything I knew to say *yes*.

While he looked at me waves hit me in reverse, and my height dropped a yard every couple of seconds. Dragon claws retracted into my hands. Scales became flesh. In a moment, I stood naked on the wet stone floor, human again.

I tested my voice, but it still didn't work. B leaned close. I stood up straight and walked up to him, feeling unstable on two legs and with such minuscule muscles. I set a hand on his snout. He made a whimpering noise.

Again I tried to speak, but my voice didn't work. I didn't seem to have a heart anymore either. I didn't have a cock or balls, but I did have a slit in this body. The dragon had made me physically human but not functionally.

He looked at the pillar and tapped it with a claw.

I shook my head and tapped B's claw, hoping he would understand I'd rather be a dragon in this place.

B was panting and struggling to stay upright. As he did, I felt my shape wavering. After a minute of struggling and gasping, he let go, and my body tingled. I stretched upward. My arms extended in another wave, green scales replacing human skin. I dropped to all fours as my body convulsed and expanded. My face elongated, and my fingers grew claws. These waves hit me fast and hard, but they felt incredibly good. So good I think I slipped out of my slit, and my cock just stayed out as I went from human to dragon. I looked between my legs, and the tip of a dragon dick poked me in the eye.

My height rapidly rose up to B's level, and then I felt normal again. B stood upright now, in relief. Keeping me in a human form took effort, but this dragon body took him no effort at all. This was my normal form. The dragon he had always desired.

I walked up to him, dick poking out between my hands. I nuzzled him. He reached up with a hand and felt my face. I lay on my dick as he felt me. My height did not drop at all.

I think he made me into the form I had been in the obsidian cave. No external blood vessels, no weird ridges, normal body proportions. Well, normal for me. I sighed in relief; I did *not* want to be a human in this place and risk a blade of grass sucking me dry of lymph or blood.

He braced one hand on the tip of my cock and licked me. I may have been projecting, but he seemed to have a thousand words on his tongue. I tried to speak again, mimicking some of the sounds I'd heard him make throughout the day.

He lowered his head.

My cock began to retract, shrinking back down to normal as he stood there, obviously under tremendous strain. Now I had to stand on my feet again.

He looked at it. My cock stopped shrinking. It began to grow again, no waves, just one smooth motion. I spread my legs apart, grinning like a human.

It reversed and began slipping back in. Disappointed but also relieved, I nuzzled him again. For the first time, I got the feeling we finally understood one another. He knew who I used to be, and that I hadn't appeared out of nowhere as an answer to all his desires. He had tested the connection between us, and he knew he could control it. If I were in his position, I'd wonder what I should do with me now.

He led me out of the cave and took flight. We flew back over many of the same landscapes, passing hundreds of mythic creatures and bizarre lands, any one of them could have been a separate country. He took me over familiar territory and then climbed back into the reflective cavern.

We walked through the tunnel together, me looking at my reflection the whole way and marveling as I watched my body move. I think I peeked from slit watching myself. Yes, I was beginning to understand the appeal of a body like this. When we set down on the floor, I wasn't sure what to do, so I rubbed flanks with B. The blue dragon rubbed me in return, and the touch made me feel real. I can't express how much that meant to me at the time. Just feeling real. B smelled so good I slipped out of my slit just being near him. This time he seemed uncertain about it. He shied away and lay on the ground.

I lay at his back, curling against him, one arm around his stomach. My muscles swelled in a sudden burst, and he pushed against me, head fitting between my pecs perfectly. He felt my arm. I wasn't even flexing, and it was tree trunk hard.

He slept. I didn't. Truthfully, I didn't feel tired. Or hungry. As that first hour passed, I wondered if I needed sleep or food anymore. I lay with my eyes open for a while, watching myself in the cave wall. I looked fierce and imposing, and yet I didn't feel that way at all.

Probably around the second hour, my body started to flicker like a candle. My scales faded into dust. I looked like a quilt coming apart at the seams and floating away in the wind. At last when my head came apart, I became a mist hanging in place over B's sleeping body.

Time seemed to pass quickly, for I watched B change positions several times, and he moved faster than he should have. My awareness waxed and waned like the moon. I wondered if my weapon had done this when I was asleep.

I don't know how much time I lost, but at some point I heard a voice. I will never forget this conversation.

"Michael? Are you there?"

Era. I saw her vague form, robes and all, standing in the cave, a shadow within a brightly lit cavern. No reflection in any of the facets.

I had no mouth, but somehow I said, "Yes, I'm here."

"You've been gone for over a month. I've been seeking out areas of concentrated magic and astral-projecting myself to them, trying to find you."

A month? I didn't realize it had been that long. "Well, here I am."

"Is everything all right?"

"Look at me!"

"I can't see you or tell exactly where you are. I can only sense your presence. What happened? Is everything all right?"

"My weapon broke while I was fighting the dragon! I'm the weapon now!"

"Can you elaborate?"

"When it broke, I felt something inside me break, too. Then I became a mist, and when I came back, I was a dragon, and now I'm bound to the dragon I had been trying to poke. I become whatever he wants me to be, and for the love of Mary he wants me to be the biggest, strongest, sluttiest[21] dragon possible."

The robed figure stood still for a moment, seeming to sink. I heard her sigh. "That is not what I hoped to hear."

"I *am* the weapon now! I can't be more than fifty yards from this dragon, and whatever he wants me to be, I become that. I think he just now figured it out. Your turn. What's happening?"

"This is bad. It shouldn't have been capable of breaking, but if it did... Michael, in order for the weapon to have whatever properties you wanted, we had to bind your soul to it."

"I know that."

---

21 Originally, the word was *whoreish*, but the connotation was not negative in M's time. Only the original sources use the older term.

"It's an easily reversible process, normally, but this was the first time anyone had tried it on an object of this kind. We were not certain how it would behave."

"Just tell me what's happening. I think my little blue friend would like to know, too."

The robed shadow sat down on a chair that wasn't there. I knew I was in for a long story, and I would not like how it ended.

"How much schooling have you had?"

"Not much. Enough to count, to sign my name, to know sign markers, and who the kings and queens of the land are."

She sighed. "All right. Try to follow this. Imagine everything around you is made of smaller things. Ancients had theories on this, and they called them 'atoms.' Individual particles too small to see. They make up our human bodies, the land, the animals, everything. Different combinations of certain elements.

"Thanks to queen Unari's patronage, we have taken the craft of magic away from intuition and conjecture and discovered method behind it. Magic has gone from a vague art to a study in precise technique, and we have discovered the source of magic: another world once called the Netherworld. We now realize it is not just mystical. It is a real place that is not made of atoms. Mystical creatures are in fact not made of the same atoms that make up humans and everything in our world. This Netherworld is their origin. When pieces of this place enter ours, they behave in strange ways. Strange but predictable. Magic. Did you know dragons and all mystical creatures cannot be killed with conventional weapons?"

"I've heard."

"Enchanted weapons are the only things that work on them, but enchantments are weak most of the time. This is because we are using only tiny fragments of their world to imbue those properties onto objects in ours. We realized if we could make an object entirely out of these particles that were not atoms, we could create something far more powerful. We have been researching ways to craft entire objects out of these *netheratoms* to give them more extraordinary abilities. That sword we gave you was the first of its kind. The first object forged entirely out of natoms. Concentrated magic in its purest form, able to take on any property we desired. We were testing how it behaved, and we hoped it would be effective not just on dragons, but anything. Nations all over the world would pay a fortune to have a weapon that could reliably kill dragons, and so that they won't need one weapon for ogres, another that only works on trolls, and so forth. Just one weapon for all creatures coming out of the Netherworld."

"Natoms?"

She laughed. "The name seems to have stuck."

I tried to laugh, too. "Your weapon worked beautifully until it broke. It cut through dragon scales like cheese."

"Well, that's *some* good news. I commend you for carrying out your mission. One moment."

The shadow disappeared for a while. B rolled over a few times, and then Era reappeared, standing this time.

"I discussed the situation with the others. Our best guess is the binding spell was the weak link. It still relied on the conventional method of enchantment, using tiny pieces of the Netherworld to link you to the weapon. When the weapon broke, the spell split between the two bound objects. They tried to reform, but in the process they reformed with you, and then the spell had no owner, so it moved to the closest person in the room. We're still not certain how the weapon retains those properties in the Netherworld. It should only be able to exist in multiple states while in the realm of atoms. It's possible our extraction of natomic particles was impure, so the weapon is capable of existing in the Netherworld in the same condition as well. You really are bound to the dragon?"

"Oh yes."

"What does he make you become? How are you coping?"

"He is one perverted lizard."

"Pardon? Never mind, our time is short. This means your body is gone, and you are now made of solid magic particles. We have a way to break natoms apart and form them into new combinations, but first we must do a soul transfer. As payment for your service, we are prepared to move you into a new body of your request. Within reason of course. No asking us to abduct kings or queens or anything like that. To do this, you will need to come back to the world of atoms."

"I don't think I can do that. B doesn't like crossing into the, uh, normal world, and I can't really communicate with him. He doesn't understand what's happening."

"I can't imagine what it's like to be bound to an animal in such a way. I am sorry this happened, but we *can* fix it."

"He's no animal."

"What do you mean?"

"He is a thinking person. I know because he's been trying to talk to me. I think all the mystical animals are. Or some of them. B took me on a tour around this place. We went to a lot of parts I recognized. We even stopped at the South Sect temple."

"You were at South Sect?"

"Yeah, we drew a crowd. I could barely see them, but they saw us. We went to other places where the two worlds kind of fade into one another."

"Interesting."

"He took me to a swamp, too. Lots of mystical animals there. They may not be animals either."

She thought for a while, seemed to listen to other people around her. "I recognize returning to us will be difficult. Seems you may be trapped there for the time being, but since we can communicate over this distance, you can help us while you're there."

"How?"

"Well, there is one thing you can do for us right now. Go back to South Sect and see if you can reach the inner sanctum."

"The inner...? I think someone mentioned that when I went there as a human. They called it the Source of Secrets. She said nobody has seen what's in there because of... something."

"Correct. It's impassable. Not only is it sealed off, but some sort of magical barrier has been set up, preventing anyone from reaching it. We in the arcane practices believe whatever is in there is the reason that temple exists halfway between our world and the Netherworld. Perhaps it is not sealed off in the other reality. Do you think you can return and investigate?"

"Yes. Yes, I think I can take us back."

"I'll send a message to South Sect and tell them to expect you. They will guide you to it. What do you look like?"

"One blue dragon and one green dragon. I'm the green one, and I'll be a mountain of muscle."

"I see. Well, this will be a good start. As a general instruction, explore as much as you can. Try to find some points of entry. This swamp you speak of. If you can find a way into it that's safe for us, it would help the field of arcane studies immensely."

"I'll try, but I can only go where B wants to go."

"Then go with him. More knowledge about the Netherworld would be useful. Have you met any other dragons?"

"Now that you mention it, no. I haven't."

"We know very little about them, so learn as much as you can. With luck, eventually you will go somewhere we can help you. I'll check in with you later. Depending on the information you provide, the queen may help us acquire a better body for your return."

"Better?"

"We'll work out the details later, but we likely will not be able to get you a human body. We could modify an animal to suit our purposes. Perhaps a cat or maybe a bird. We could also move you into a suit of armor or an automaton. Something that would allow you to live among men again."

"I'll try."

"Good. Again, I am sorry this happened, but perhaps we can turn a tragedy into a triumph. Be safe, Michael."

The shadow vanished. I remained vapor floating about the cave, but now feeling immense relief not being so alone anymore, and... you have your dick out. Is that a hint? Oh, you all have your dicks out. Well, I guess that means it's time for a break. Come here. I'll suck you off if you rub me.[22]

---

22 Here, a number of scribes wrote in the margins of their manuscripts: *I just got fucked by a dragon. Can't believe I'm being paid to do this. / He loves dick in his ass. Ancient stories never said dragons could be good lays. / I think I'm in love with M's dick. / His body is a delight to explore. It's different every time I feel it.*

SESSION 4

I was afraid this would be boring. I didn't expect to meet nine people who were just like me. Do all scribes like dick?[23] Do all scribes want to fuck a dragon?[24]

Well, let's get back to it. I later learned B was asleep for four days. Dragons are awake for a month straight and then sleep for up to a week. I knew B woke up when I changed from a mist back into a solid body, a mountain of green muscle on four legs. B remained on his side, eyes closed.

His scent was worthy of worship. As soon as I had a physical body again, my nose took me straight to his slit and I inhaled. I instantly slipped out of my slit and drenched the cave floor with clear fluid. It echoed as it fell.

B lay still, eyes closed, but definitely awake. I licked him once. B shifted and grunted. I scented him again. B raised a leg wider, and that was all I needed; I shoved my muzzle in there and licked as hard as I could. I felt his dick poking my snout and let it emerge. I ran my tongue over it as it grew. It stopped midway up his stomach, and I kept licking. Deliciously slick and pungent. Tasting it made my own slit drip.

After a few minutes licking him from base to tip, B rolled over to his back and spread his legs. He opened his

---

23 *Not all, but most of the ones I've met. It's a secret of our Guild.*

24 *His dick is gorgeous, and his legs are as thick as my whole body.*

eyes, and on sight, I grew again. Arms, chest, legs, wings. Everything on me except my cock. I moved over him and lay on top of him. I continued expanding, chest pushing him harder against the ground.

He reached up and felt my arms all the way up to my shoulders. Nothing yielded to his touch. He felt the lines running down my shoulders, making my triceps. He explored every crevice on each pectorals, and I gave him a show, moving the muscles every way I could, making them pucker.

I needed it badly, and I had become exactly what he wanted, so I angled my dick just under his slit and nudged him.

He leaned forward, felt the muscles in my neck. I pushed in. He spread his legs wider and grunted. I held him down harder and slid in the rest of the way.

Either he had done this before, or dragons are just naturally loose. This was so much easier than when I had done it as a human. No need to carry lard or oil with me; my body makes its own, and it must have made a lot because I went in with no effort.

My hips tingled, and my dick grew in a wave from the base to the tip. B held me close, mouth open but no sounds coming out of it. His own dick leaked against my stomach. My hips tingled again, and my height rose another yard. My legs grew another yard as well, and they bulged outward.

I thrust him gently, worried he had made me grow too large to handle. My dick remained usable, and I felt the barbs and ridges rubbing him. I'd fucked men before, but this was a whole other experience.

As I worked him, he made me grow even bigger. Not the dick, but the rest of me. Always in cascading waves that began at the hips. I was so thick I don't think I could have walked, but I didn't need to. I stood up on my forelegs as I lay buried in his ass, giving him a full view of my underside, along with the arms pushing against my chest muscles. I let him see them in motion as I thrust him.

He turned his head and looked at us in the obsidian walls. I think he blew a load just watching me fuck him. I could smell it now, and it made me grow again. Now I turned and looked at myself. I towered over him, three times his size, and so muscular my chest had become all he could see now.

I grew a little more every time I pushed into him, growling, roaring, adjusting my stance every three waves as my height rose and my stance widened. When I finally finished, I worried I would hurt him. He held my arms as I filled him up.

I think it was almost a minute before I finished cumming, and when I pulled out, I was still leaking. I drenched him in my seed. I noticed his stomach had swollen a little. He reached up with all four limbs and held my dick as it continued squirting him, closing his eyes and grunting.

I loomed over him, making sure he could see my muscles next time he opened his eyes. Now my dick grew into something more proportional to my body, and I grunted with him as he made me grow, hoping to tell him how amazing this felt.

Finally I lay on top of him and licked his snout. My muzzle was twice the size of his now, and he held my face as he licked my nose. I licked him back, lapping up my own seed, which tasted sweet. I wondered if dragons normally had sweet jizz or if this was just how he wanted me to taste.

I rose to all four feet and stood over him. He was covered in my jizz, and I had his scent all over me. My dick was still out and pulsing, now as thick as B's whole body and dripping lube. I hoped he understood I enjoyed this, too, and I wanted him to make me into whatever he wanted.

Best sex I[25] ever had, either with a man or a woman.

He rolled to his feet, feeling his swollen stomach. My nose took me under his tail, and I licked him. When I was human, I never would have done this, but tasting our scents mixed together was like drinking cider.

I thought I would indulge him again, so I raised a hand and pushed him down to the ground. He held his tail as high as it could go, and I licked the scents off him.

I don't remember how we ended up outside. I must have been drunk on our mixed scents, or maybe he fell asleep and I turned into a vapor again and didn't become solid until he calmed down.

I stood at a normal height again, but I had a hard time moving. My muscles hadn't shrunk much. I liked being this big, and he seemed to like me this way, too. I noticed his belly wasn't swollen anymore.

Now I was on my back, and he was feeling me up. I hoped he would fuck me, but the only way I could tell him so was to spread my legs as far apart as possible. He noticed, and I felt pressure under my tail. I must have held him so tight he couldn't breathe. Good to know I really was as strong as I looked, and these muscles weren't just decoration.

I felt every inch of his dick in me. For the first time since the weapon broke, I felt whole. I wanted to swallow him so I'd never be without this feeling. He made me grow as he fucked me, and he never seemed to tire of feeling my chest and abs. I sprawled out, letting him feel my arms, too. He could not get enough of me, and I wanted him to stay inside me forever.

---

25 Some manuscripts render this as *I'd*. It is one of multiple typographical discrepancies between the original sources.

I caught some new smells. I looked around and saw dragon shapes in the distance. Outlines, shadows. What's the word? Silhouettes. In the daylight. One sitting on a mountain peak. Another peeking up from a cluster of tentacle trees. I saw six figures watching us. I couldn't see any scales. Just shadowy outlines, and occasionally the wind would bring a scent to me. I tried to alert B about them, but he didn't notice; too busy fucking me to look around.

I didn't blame him. He felt amazing inside me, and here I was this giant dragon lying helpless under him, pinned down by his dick. He seemed to like that.

While he worked my ass, I noticed three more dragon silhouettes watching us. B seemed to be more here at the moment, so I tapped him on the muzzle with a claw. He looked at me. I gestured with my snout toward one of the shadows, and he looked up.

Three more shadows. Watching us. I wanted to ask B how they could see us from so far away, and should we be worried or switch to a more presentable position?

B pulled out and nudged me, so I rolled over and crouched on all fours, wings spread. B mounted me and shoved it back in. I had to crouch lower so he could lie on my back. I kept my wings up so the onlookers could see how thick my arms were. I deliberately flexed them so they'd push my chest out. I lowered my head on one of his deep thrusts and took a peek between my legs. My dick wasn't too far out of proportion right now; just up to my forelegs and about half as a thick. Probably the closest it's ever been to normal size, if B was normal. The barbs flared every time B thrust.

I expected to grow, but I must have been big enough for him. He was certainly enough for me. His barbs hit all the right places.[26] I drenched the grass in seed. Several min-

---

26 *M's barbs feel like God Himself rubbing your insides.*

utes later, B sped up, and then he emptied himself into me. I got far more out of it than I expected. When he filled me up... It's hard to explain. I felt more *together*. Not a human stretched into a dragon's body, but a dragon that had outgrown his human body.

He climbed off me, dick hanging, still shooting, flared barbs lining the tip and parts of the shaft. Was about as long as his front leg and half as thick. I slipped my head under his belly and licked it. No taste. Apparently being made of magic meant I had no entrails. Only what B wanted me to have.

I followed his dick as it retracted to his slit. I teased his slit a little and then came up, forgetting I stood taller and thrice as bulky.

He looked around. Our audience had vanished. B said some things, but the grunts and growls meant nothing to me. From his posture, I gathered that change in his scent meant he was nervous.

I bumped flanks with him, fluttering my wings, hoping dragons used that as a playful gesture. He continued looking around, anxiously. I bumped him again, and this time he pushed me back. He couldn't even move me, and I liked feeling solid as a boulder.

He backed away and spread his wings. I spread mine, ready to follow him, but he didn't take off. Instead he looked at me and then swung his neck out. I hoped it meant he wanted me to lead this time, so I took off and started flying. As I hoped, he brought up the rear.

I knew exactly where I wanted to go. I wished I could have explained why, but for now, I hoped he had a sense that I had been to places in his world as a human, and I wanted to see them from this side. They did seem to be clearer and less dangerous now that I had a magical body. I remembered how to get there. Some weird new sense I had acquired. One hell of a map in my head. I could practically count the number of wingstrokes[27] it would take to reach it.

I landed on the bottom mesa, and B landed next to me, swinging his neck and puffing little jets of fire from his nose, amused I'd want to come back to South Sect.

I hadn't needed to clean up. My scales had absorbed all the jizz, and even my ass seemed to be empty. B's scent had returned to normal, but still pungent. Went straight to my groin. The last time we did this, he had calmed down for a while. Not this time; I started dripping from my slit, leaving a trail of lube everywhere I went. I hoped the barrier between the world of atoms and the world of, uh, natoms—I wish they could come up with a better word— was more solid. I didn't want anyone to slip on this stuff. You've felt it. Imagine leaving a trail of that around a stone floor.[28] I wanted it to stop, but I didn't think B considered it something that needed to. In fact, I caught him sniffing it behind me, and it made him peek from his slit. I would later learn dragons consider it a sign of virility, and he wanted nothing if not that.

Anyway, I remembered where the main entrance to the place was, so I led us there, catching glimpses of people walking about. Some of them followed us. I heard echoes of chants. I remembered these chants from when I had visited as a human. I had laughed then, but no laughing now that I knew they weren't just chanting at shadows on the wall.

I paused at the entrance and gestured, wondering if B had ever been inside. He didn't seem afraid of this place.

From the corner of my eye, I saw robed men and women lining up and looking at me, pointing deeper into

---

27 Some manuscripts hyphenate this word, but most of the original sources do not.

28 Archaeologists have found the ruins of this temple, and they have noted such staining on the floor. Some out of the way places still have liquid resting on them. Centuries later, it is still slippery.

the temple. I walked down the slope, B following, sniffing and sometimes licking up the trail I was leaving. I laughed inwardly thinking we'd have no problem finding our way back out.

As a human, I had never been allowed this way. I had been confined to a specific chamber, and that's where I conducted all business with the Sect. Now this same Sect guided me down ramps and corridors, pointing down this branch instead of the other. I wondered if B could see these people. I looked back from time to time, and B seemed more interested in the trail of lube I was leaving. I caught him watching my thighs. My ass in motion. I didn't mind.

We must have descended a hundred fathoms. Fewer and fewer people were around to point the way, and to my surprise, at one point, B walked ahead of me and took the lead for the rest of the journey.

Then we came to a place where the air felt so thick it seemed like a solid wall. I looked at it in my... what's it called? Peripheral vision, thanks, and I saw a wall of air that looked like stone. On my side, the one not made of atoms, it looked like thick air, but not solid.

B walked straight through this barrier. So did I. We must have been under the mountain, for the cavern opened up into a mountain-shaped cavity made of air so thick I could almost walk on it.

Lying in the middle of this cavity, I saw a dragon large enough to dwarf an entire city and its people. She could have swallowed a neighborhood of people whole. She could have squashed a hundred houses under a single foot. Her purple and white scales glowed, and her presence seemed to pull me toward her. Physically. I caught myself sliding, as if on a downhill slope, but this chamber was flat earth.

I stared.

B had turned and looked at me. He coughed a little ball of fire on me. Did he know about this place? He must have been here before; he turned around again and walked straight up to her thigh—holy shit just one claw could have crushed B completely. I just crouched there like a terrified dog, looking at her. And yes, I knew the dragon was a she. I could tell the scents apart by now.

I had slid forward about twenty steps without realizing it. Again, not on a downhill, and I had to back away just to remain standing still.

A sound filled this cave. I realized it was her breath. She was asleep.

B had now taken flight and was moving straight to her. Had I been human, I wouldn't have been able to see him; he was so small compared to her, but I followed him with my eyes.

He landed on her thigh, smaller than a flea on a dog's hide. I shivered where I stood and backed away to stay standing there. B opened his mouth and flamed her.

I screamed. Mother of God, I screamed like a baby. I think I would have pissed myself if I'd had any piss in me, but instead more lube came out.

B could obviously still see me, and he laughed. He took flight again, blowing flames up her leg, across her back. It took several minutes for him to fly up her back and reach her head, and now he flamed across the top of her head.

I shivered and screamed again, trying to back away.

She continued to snooze.

I watched her eye, easily as large as a few castles—ten of B could have fit inside it. It never opened.

B perched on the crown of her head and roared, belching flames everywhere. My legs twitched, and I backed away to the barrier. The binding spell between us stretched taut, but I fought it, hoping to pull him down. I turned and ran through the entrance. To the few humans on the other side, halfway between the world of atoms and the world of natoms, I must have looked like a ghost coming through a solid wall.

They knelt when they saw me. I probably looked like I had seen the devil himself in there. I tried to warn them, and my inability to form human words made me so furious I tried to roar, but it came out as a pathetic squeak.

Minutes later, I felt the spell relax, and then B rested his head on top of mine. He was grumbling, trying to talk to me, making reassuring sounds.

Once I composed myself, I jumped to my feet and followed my lube trail straight up and out of that place with B right behind me, trying to keep up. For being so muscular my thighs rubbed together and my arms squeezed my chest all the time, I could move quick.

In no time, I had burst out of the temple and taken flight. B flew beside me, banking left and right, scent carefree. I noticed he flew with his dick hanging out. He had been watching me run from behind the whole time, watching those muscles at work, slit dripping lube. In fact, his muzzle was drenched in it, and he licked it as he flew beside me.

I could barely stay in the air, and I eventually dropped to a place in a field of thorny vines grew. No flowers. Just vines. The thorns didn't even scratch my scales, and I stood up to my stomach in them, shaking like a baby rabbit.

B landed in front of me and grunted. I gestured over my shoulder and then covered my eyes with a hand.

The blue dragon snorted a little flame over my face and batted me on the side of the snout with one hand. I figured he had just given me the dragon's gesture for *chin up*.

I tried to picture her standing here, and I couldn't even imagine a dragon that size existing. I stood panting for several minutes. I must have started pacing. It felt like I should have been lightheaded, but I wasn't. I think I was trying to make myself feel lightheaded and sick because that was the only way to react. I didn't feel those things anymore. Took me a while to realize that.

When I stopped, I saw I had trampled the vines enough to make a clearing, and B was sitting on his haunches, just looking at me. He wasn't hard, but he was looking me up and down. Beholding is a better word, yeah, he *beheld* me. He seemed short of breath. I tried to smile. I knew what I looked like, and I'd been walking around in front of him, shoulders bulging as they held up my weight, neck rippling. B was drinking in the sight, and he wasn't out of his slit this time.

That's when I realized I didn't feel physically overwhelmed. I stood up straight and marched back and forth a few times, this time watching B. He had to remind himself to breathe once in a while. I couldn't giggle the way I was used to. I couldn't even snort to imitate laughter or a smile. All I could think to do was strut back and forth in front of him. I expected something on me to get bigger. Nothing happened.

I spread my wings, looking up at them. Like a third pair of arms hanging over me, muscles just as thick as my forelegs. They looked weird to me, but B was captivated. I faced him and fanned him with my wings. He scented the air. I turned and puckered my chest a few times for him. Those were more familiar muscles, and honestly it felt really good to have muscles large enough to show off like this. Hired swords tend to be lean. We have to be to fit through windows and slip away quickly. Being big was a novelty. And honestly it was fun.

I sat down and held an arm out, looking it over. I wanted to feel for myself how thick it was, so I tried to reach over, but my chest was in the way. B really liked that sight. He peeked from his slit, just a little. I grunted and bent my arm, making the muscles squish together, gesturing to it with my snout.

B launched from his seat and wrapped his hands around my arm. I couldn't feel it myself, so he felt it for me, and as he did I made sure to show him I liked being touched. I adjusted my stance to open myself up for his hand to wander, and he wandered over to my chest and up my neck. This made me feel less like a human and more like a flying lizard from the Netherworld.

Humans... Muscular necks just don't exist for us. It's something only dragons admire, and I made some grunting noises to let B know he could feel my neck up and down all day if he wanted. I wished I could have told him I didn't feel solid unless he touched me.

My companion barely breathed the whole time he felt me up. He really liked the shoulders and my bulging chest —he must have spent a good quarter hour feeling every peak and valley of those. I sat still and worked those muscles as he ran his fingers over and between them. I showed him I couldn't feel my own arms they were so big and my chest stuck out that far, and he responded by trying to push my arms together. It only made my chest bigger, and he couldn't get enough of this.

Having drank in my entire upper body with his hands and his snout, he stood right in front of me, only slightly shorter. He used my chest to pull himself up to me, and he felt my muzzle. He scented my breath.

I reached back and felt his snout. I scented his breath, too, as I felt his face all the way down his neck to the shoulder.

I had to be sure, so I held my other arm out and gestured to it. He rested a hand on the bicep. I flexed it, made his fingers spread out. Grunting, I nuzzled him. B seemed to brighten. I hoped he understood he could feel these whenever he wanted, and I didn't mind if he gawked.

I remember thinking his breath smelled beautiful when I noticed the land was fading to yellow. B noticed, too, and he broke away from me. Seconds later, we were standing on a yellow field of nothing. Not dirt. Just the color. Nothing grew anywhere as far as I saw. No features. No ups or downs, no hills.

Dragons were now all around us, emerging from the air. I recognized these scents: all the same people who had watched me and B fuck earlier. Eleven dragons surrounded us, and nobody cast a shadow. I took comfort knowing that B did not smell scared. I stood straight and tried to be brave.

Something about them... They had strange scents. That's when I noticed they had things stuck between their scales. At first I thought they were jewels, because they sparkled and some of them shined in my eyes no matter how I looked at them, but then I realized these things were just rocks. Ordinary stones you'd find on the side of the road, polished and rounded and somehow embedded in scales all up and down their bodies. Not embedded. *Replacing* scales! It looked so weird to see river rocks and garden stones breaking up otherwise beautiful and fierce-looking blood red and ghost white and olive black reptile skin.

B sat on his haunches. He glanced at me, and I did the same. I couldn't help but notice B peeking from his slit. I leaked from mine more than ever, and I sat deliberately making sure my arms puckered my chest out. My pecs stuck out so far I couldn't see my feet without craning my neck, and even the muscles on my neck seemed to brush against my shoulders.

I stood taller than a few of these dragons. Most seemed awed by my size. I stared at one particular dragon who had deep red scales that faded to olive around her belly, a line of round river rocks running up her body and, I guessed, bisecting it.

Soundlessly, the yellow land fell away everywhere a person was not, and normal-looking features faded in where the flat color had been. Each dragon now stood perched on a column of rock that stretched far, far below and ended in an ocean. B and I stood on a tiny platform of rock as well, probably another column of our own.

I had been in court before. I hoped B made for a good lawyer.

They started talking. Grunts and growls and chirps, all overlapping each other. Broad sweeps of the neck, cutting the air with claws, B walking around me on our tiny platform, facing this person and that person.

I stood as regal[29] as possible, but I flinched when one of them flicked his hands and mumbled something. A beam of light shot from his hand and hit me in the chest. I sat still, waiting for something to happen.

B continued to circle me and speak to them. More of them chanted things, and the rocks in their scales lit up and pulsed. I felt energy rising like a thunderstorm, and clouds of mist appeared over some of these Judges.

More beams hit me, and I looked, but nothing else happened. I sat still and took it as B watched, taking great care not to be in the way.

One of the Judges rose to all fours and swiped the air with his claws. The stones embedded in his skull and ringing his hands lit up, and the entire landscape swirled around like a whirlpool and vanished, leaving all of us in a field of vines again. Somehow the Judges did not seem to be here. The light from the sun did not hit them the same, and their colors seemed off compared to me and B.

---

29 Some of the original sources record this as *regally*.

One of them grunted something in B's direction, and then they all swiped their claws, cutting through the air itself and tearing it. They walked into these tears and vanished.

I rose to all fours and looked at B. He swung around and stood flank to flank with me, rubbing his neck against mine. I couldn't believe he hadn't made me grow or something to impress those dragons.

He pranced ahead of me like a cat and spread his wings. I spread mine in anticipation. He took us in a different direction from the South Sect temple and the swamp. We flew for a long time, passing more strange plants and oceans of bizarre colors.

We finally came to a city. Now try to imagine a city made of bones that does not look menacing. To us, bones mean death, but to dragons, bones mean life, so bridges and walkways were made of dragon bones. Where they got so many, I still have no idea, but buildings made of fingers, homes made of skulls and legs and arms and wings, and yet none of it looked terrifying or foreboding. This city looked bright and full of life, and it was filled with dragons of all shapes and sizes, none of whom had rocks embedded in their scales.

Finally, normal dragons in a normal place. When we landed, people looked at us. B gave sounds and gestures I assumed were greetings, as the other dragons around returned them and went about their business. I couldn't quite make out what everyone was doing. In normal cities, I'd expect merchants to be selling meats and vegetables and jewels and weapons, and scribes to be carrying scrolls and books about and making ink. All of those things I associated with cities.

These dragons in the Netherworld... Some carried blobs of glowing green gel in their mouths. Others had their necks down wells, also made of bones, and came up with slimy eels that seemed to be made of light. Nobody ate the things; they carried them about and deposited them on the bones, and the eels slithered between them.

I saw other dragons emerging from what I can only describe as a house. As one, they turned and faced the house. They chanted, and the bones making up the house shifted and rearranged themselves into a different kind of house. The dragons then moved on. Some continued to chant. The bones behind them shifted and adjusted position.

I glared at B. My dragon lover bumped noses with me and led me into the city. I had only seen the outskirts. The big buildings lay ahead.

I expected to see people at work. The dragons I saw as we walked were doing things that looked like anything but. Some were singing to globs of gel, which sank into the pathway made of tiny wing bones. These people greeted us as we passed. I did my best to return the greeting. I caught whiffs of hormones as we passed. Lots of dragons were impressed by my size.

We passed a few dragons who were tearing into some animal I did not recognize, but it appeared to be made of many different kinds of animals. It did not bleed blood, but some sort of dust fell from its gaping wounds. The dragons were eating this dust. They waved muzzles at us as they crunched on that powder. It didn't smell like bone or blood or anything I recognized.

I noticed I had been leaving a trail of slit juice the whole time we walked. The other dragons seemed impressed. I stood as tall as I could, but right then I would rather have gone back on trial. I felt more comfortable in court than here.

I noticed a few dragons less than a quarter my size—children, obviously—standing on a field of flat bones off the path of bumpy ones B and I walked on. One blew fire onto something, and the shiny thing returned sparks. The children pranced in glee. Another clawed it and backed away. The thing shot about a yard off the ground and twirled.

It was a hammer.

I paused and blinked as the children played with it, treating it like this dangerous object, but none of the adults around seemed to care, so it couldn't have been a real threat.

Another young dragon stomped it with both hands. It sent sparks out, and the child tried to hold it down. The others seemed to encourage him to endure this, and then she stepped off, and the thing twitched and sparked about. The children leaped around it, snorting little jets of flame in all directions.

I galloped to catch up to B, drawing some stares as other dragons nearby noticed my thighs rubbing together and how far my chest stood out and how many abdominals I had.

I saw so much more, and none of it made sense. By the time we reached what I could only call the city proper, I could barely see straight, and I felt so confused I wanted to go back to the obsidian cave.

Towers of bones. Dragons flew into and out of them, like an inn hundreds of yards high, made of smoothed bones, with hundreds of holes. I saw some dragons perched inside these holes. I heard roars and calls, and B answered them with similar calls.

B flew up one of these towers. I followed him as he circled it up and around, and then entered one of these cavities. I followed him and perched inside. A room at an inn, but the smooth bones curved and flowed to make places to sit and lie down. Room for three dragons our size. Nice place, actually.

B walked around, showed me *this* place was for sitting, *this* place was formed to allow you to stand but take the weight off your feet, *this* place was molded as a bed. I imitated his positions at the various places, and I fit, bulky as I was.

The bed looked the most interesting. Room for two, a bowl of bone. I deduced B had been out to seek a partner, and now he'd found one, so he qualified for a place like this. The best I could figure at the time, yet it didn't explain why he had been so far out, and in a cave by himself, but right now, B lay in the bowl. I lay on the other side, and we ended up curling into one another.

So... dragon society.

I had a feeling even if I could speak their language I wouldn't understand a thing.

He did not sleep. We just cuddled for a while. I didn't turn to vapor, but I did see a shadowy, robed figure projected on the curved wall of this egg-shaped cavity in the bone tower.

"What did you see in there?" Era asked.

I did not even want to think about South Sect. I didn't speak in words. I just thought, and she seemed to receive my meaning. "There's a dragon in there. She's huge. Big. Enormous. Gigantic! The mountain is hollow, and she fills it! She'd swallow a village whole!"

"They told me you left in a hurry, so scared you outran your friend even in the air."

"I'm not kidding! There's a giant dragon asleep in the mountain near that temple."

"She's asleep? That's strange. Records of South Sect go back three thousand years. Even the earliest records show the area fades between the two worlds. Has the dragon been there all this time?"

"I don't know. And I think I met the leaders of their society. They put me on trial. They shot magic at me."

"Magic? The dragons were using magic?"

"Their mages had rocks embedded in their scales. Those rocks glowed, and they cast spells. I swear they were just ordinary rocks, like you'd find in gardens or slingshots. And now I'm in a dragon city, and I saw some dragon children playing with a damn carpenter's hammer! It was dancing around and sparking and jumping when they poked it. What in the name of the queen is happening?"

"Dragon city?"

"Made of bones. The entire thing. The fields are smooth. The paths are bumpy—I can see individual arms and legs and wings and skulls. People are doing things, but I can't even describe what. Me and B are in a tower made of smooth bone. Our room is sculpted right into the side, and the furniture is part of the walls and floor. I don't know what we're supposed to do now. Era, did the ancients write about any of this?"

"No. All of this is new to us. Nobody has ever been in the Netherworld deep enough or long enough to see any of this, let alone return to tell the tale. Let's deal with it one thing at a time. South Sect is built near a giant, sleeping dragon."

"I can't comprehend how anything can be that big. B didn't seem worried at all. He laughed at me for being scared."

"That implies its presence is common knowledge among dragons, and it is of no concern to them."

"She is the source of that area being halfway between worlds. I'm sure of it. I saw nothing out of the corner of my eye in there. That cave is completely in the Netherworld, and the further out you go, the less of our world I could see."

"I'll pass that along to the others. You say dragons also practice magic?"

"Something like it, yes."

"With garden rocks?"

"I swear on my loins they had normal, ordinary rocks in their skin, and those things glowed with power. Lightning shot from them."

"I may have a partial explanation for that. Atoms probably behave strangely in the Netherworld, just as natoms behave in unusual ways in ours. They're garden rocks in our world, but they may be conduits of power in theirs. So dragons have mages, too."

"What does it mean?"

"It's too soon to draw conclusions. We know of five other sites similar to South Sect. Areas where our world and theirs blur. I need you to go to at least one of them and tell me if you find another dragon of this size. If so, we will know this is deliberate."

She told me four more places I could go, none of which I had been to before. I told her I'd visit one as soon as possible. I wanted to know, too.

"Now what?"

"Michael, every mage in Hirinda is following this. Everyone is researching and proposing ideas every step of the way. If dragons practice magic, and that giant you saw is not unique, then it has a purpose, and we must find out what. Keep exploring. We're working on figuring out what it means. On a personal note, how are you holding up?"

I sent her laughter and said, "I think I'm married now."

"Married?"

"B and I just moved into a tower, and we have our own little alcove. The mages of this world must have approved of me, so now we're together. We're in a nest made of bone.

He seems quite happy, and damn he smells nice, even while sleeping."

"I'm sure *he* does."

"Oh, sorry, I thought I mentioned it before."

She laughed. "We are aware of your crimes against nature."

I didn't know how to respond, so I just said, "Uh..."

"You have a bit of a reputation among mercenaries. That's how we found out about you, and why we chose you for this assignment. We figured if someone had to handle an untested weapon made of untested magic, it should be someone who is not aligned well with the Church."

"Sure. If I died, no loss."

"You understand our queen is aligned with the Church, and we receive funding from the queen. I personally don't care what you do in the woods, and now it seems to have come in handy."

"Lucky me, I happen to be just as perverted as he is, and honestly, I am loving this. He is a damn good lay. Likes his men big. Big everywhere."

"South Sect told me you were the bulkiest dragon they ever glimpsed. I wish I could see. I am glad to know it suits you. Well, as the only human witness to your marriage, I wish you God's blessing, and with a little luck your marriage will last longer than mine did."

"You were married?"

"Years and years ago. My parents pressured me to marry him. Told me there's no place for a woman without a husband. They were right, but they married me off to a man who hated women."

"Hated? How so?"

"Long story. Maybe I'll tell you sometime. For now I'll say I began learning magic in case I had to kill him."

"Drunken rage?"

"Actually, no. He wasn't a drinker. I think he just hated that he had to be married, so he hated me. The mages took me in after I fled. So glad we didn't have any children. No hurry on the other locations. Learn as much as you can about dragon magic. Dragon society as well. The more you can tell us, the better our chances of figuring out what's happening. I must go now. Be safe, Michael."

"Thanks, Era."

The shadow on the bone wall faded to white, and I...

Ready for another dose of dragon seed? Yes, I know I slipped out of my sheath an hour ago. You've been staring at my throbbing dicks for a while, so you deserve a reward, and then we'll call it a day.[30]

---

30 B gave him four cocks this time, as thick as my arm. Four of us sucked him at once, and he didn't go soft after finishing; he was ready and eager for four more immediately after, and then he fucked us. I hope this story never ends. Too bad B can't join us in here. Sometimes he pokes his head in, but mostly he doesn't disturb us.

SESSION 5

I wish I'd have found the scribes when I was younger. You might've persuaded me to join instead of becoming a sword for hire.[31]

Then again, I wouldn't be here if I had. I wouldn't have these, which I notice all of you can't stop staring at.[32]

I refuse to wear clothes, even in the presence of royalty. B is an artist, and I am his sculpture, and I will never cover up his work.

So we're at the bone tower. We don't sleep, but now that we're alone and out of sight, I grow. I knew it was coming, so I rolled over and cuddled against him. The wave began there and stretched me out. B opened his eyes and watched. He held my arm and my body expanded again. My arm was now twice as thick as his neck.

He fit comfortably between my arms. I knew even then he had grown me so he would fit there, for my chest and stomach conformed to his body perfectly. I pulled him close, and he buried his muzzle in my chest. Hidden, actually. I flexed my chest, squeezing his face. He ran his hands up the back of my arms.

He smelled good.

------

31 *His muscles are bigger today, but his frame is not. They bunch up and push against one another even while seated in his special chair. How can he move?*

32 *He flexed his arms. They dwarfed his head. We asked him if they were real. He crushed a block of marble with his bare hands. His chest and shoulders still haven't shrunk from the effort. We were all hard before we even began.*

I reached down and teased his slit. We were both leaking lube, and he was already out of his slit, feeling my abdominal muscles with his cock. His barbs had flared, and I felt every single one of them. No, really, my sense of touch was so sharp I could probably have counted the legs on a fly that landed on me. All my senses were sharp beyond imagining.

I pushed him up against the side of the bowl. He lifted a leg. I felt air hitting my cock, and I pushed in. I don't know how big he made my dick, but it slid in with no effort, and he held me under my forelegs as he took me to the hilt.

He kept his wings folded as I thrust him. I fanned mine. I got the feeling he wasn't in the mood for a hard fuck. Neither was I; I just liked being close to him. Something about becoming whatever he wanted. Being able to fuck on command. No preparation, no foreplay, no talking. Just sniff his slit and you know he's ready. Dragons have it made, let me tell you. Scent-based societies have none of the problems humans have. None. No forcing people to be together for family reasons. If their scent is right, you know they're right for you, and his scent...

Sorry. I felt him finish on my stomach, and his hands wandered down from my shoulders to my chest. I felt solid, and I wanted to show him, so I tightened my whole body for him. He pressed against me harder. I held him close to me, making sure he saw my arms in motion. He couldn't be close enough to me. I didn't know much about dragons, but when it came to sex, they seemed to like the same things humans did.

I kept my thrusts deep and held him as tight as I could. I think I could have blown a load just from his scent.

He nudged me, and I rolled to my back. He sat on me, and now I saw that while I had grown, my dick had remained normal-sized. Probably looked a bit strange, but now he had an unobstructed view of me. I spread my arms and my wings out, filling the bowl and much of our alcove. He braced himself on my chest and rode me a few times. I raised my arms and showed them in motion, and he leaned over me and felt my chest, and then his hands migrated around my arms.

I pushed in. He responded by riding me. I noticed he was out of his slit again. I wanted to lean forward and suck him, but my pecs were too thick for me to lean forward. All I could do was stick my snout between them and flick my tongue.

Then I grew again. My head touched the edge of the bowl, and my wings curled over us. He kept riding, hands feeling my tight stomach all the down to my thighs. I lowered my arms and let them become part of the wall that was my torso.

Just the sight of it made him finish. It covered my chest, and I stuck my tongue between my pecs to get it.

Tasting him pushed me over the edge. I grabbed him around his wings and pulled him into me. His muzzle fit perfectly between my pecs, now wet with his seed, and I started thrusting him harder. I roared when I finished. He lit up. Took me a moment to realize he had breathed fire all over me. He was feeling my chest as I pumped him full of seed.

He sat up and pulled out. To my surprise, my dick had grown. I leaned over to see it, but again my chest prevented me from moving too far forward. My dick was half as thick as his whole body.

I embraced him. He had already curled up on me, using my chest as pillows. Moments later, I faded into vapor, and he sank down to the bowl gently, sleeping so deep I don't think he would have woken up if the tower had fallen over.

Now I got to watch society go by while he slept. Dragons flew around. Some of them hovered in front of our alcove and then took off. I wondered if they saw me in here. A lone dragon asleep, or a lone dragon asleep under a cloud of mist? Did I fill the cavity?

I wondered if I could move around like this, so I tried moving to the window, or entrance, or whatever it should be called. I don't have the words to describe how I did this. I kind of just gathered myself up and moved, and the rest of me followed. I didn't want to go too far outside; I was afraid I would be caught in the wind and blown away.

Time passed much faster than I expected. A number of dragons peeked inside our alcove. A few perched on the lip and looked in. One of them stood inside my cloud. She didn't seem to notice me at all, which meant even dragons couldn't tell I existed when not solid.

The sun went down, but the light here only changed from daylight to deep red. It made the bones look surreal. Shadows became elongated. It reminded me of harvest season. From the window, I observed dragons walking and flying about. Many of them were engaged in tasks, but even when watching from this vantage point I didn't understand them.

One pair of dragons were flying around the next tower in opposing spirals, one breathing fire over it, the other sneezing some kind of power on it. I watched them cover the entire tower from bottom to top like this, and when they were done, I saw no difference.

I saw other dragons walking about. Had they been in human society, I would have expected to see a marketplace, but none of these creatures did that. Let me go out of sequence for a moment and tell you when everyone can fly and hunt for themselves, society will center around different things. Dragon society is very much like that, but I didn't understand it then.

I observed lots and lots of dragons walking about. One of them gave a small pebble of basalt to another dragon, and then walked off. No exchange of money. No obvious reason. The black dragon who now had the pebble slipped it into a hole in her horn, obviously carved to hold a rock of this size. She glowed a little.

Dragons singing to blobs of blue gel. These blobs sank into the ground, and the bones on the path smoothed out and became a flat sheet of white. Very weird to see hundreds of arm and leg and wing bones, along with skulls and horns and fingers and spines liquefy and become a polished plane.

Dragons walked on the bumpy paths. They stayed off the smooth areas. It seemed to be law, but what were all these dragons with the blobs doing changing path areas to smooth? And why would dragons walk anywhere when they could fly everywhere?

More time passed, and then suddenly I become solid again, back to typical size for me. I turned around, letting my thick tail dangle from the alcove, and sat regally while B awoke. He looked like a little bird swimming in a soup bowl, and I wanted to pick him up and keep him under my hat for safe keeping.

His scent had become even more intense. I peeked from my slit. I made sure to stand so my arms puffed my chest. When he turned around, I was the first thing he saw. He rolled to all fours and walked up to me. He licked me from my slit all the way up to my chin. I grunted in approval. He cooed.

We left our alcove, and I followed him down to the path. We walked on spines and legs and arms, and I looked around like a damn tourist.

Everyone was doing something, but most of it I couldn't understand. Somewhere along the way, I noticed each building had a rock overhead. One of those river rocks I'd seen embedded into the Judges' scales earlier.

I looked back at our tower, and sure enough I saw a few pebbles of granite suspended over its roof. Yes, suspended. I couldn't tell how or what kept it overhead, but it looked so wrong.

Long story short, we became two of those gel-singers. B led us to a building, which had a fragment of marble over it, and we both took a hunk of liquid that somehow stayed together with no container, and we went around singing to the different buildings. The gel melted into the buildings, and the bones changed. Then the blob came back and we went to another building. I didn't know what I was doing, so I just imitated whatever song B made. We did this for hours, then B led us to the office, we gave our blob back, and we went home.

I felt weirdly accomplished.

B sat in the "chair" for a while, head between two plates of what looked like bone. I watched, puzzled, and then I noticed we had room for two. I rested in this other space and stuck my head between the plates.

I heard sounds coming from it. Grunting and growling. Voices with no source. I listened for a while, not understanding a word, but B reacted from time to time, so whatever they were saying, it must have been informative. Or funny.

I got up when he got up, and he led us in flight out of the city and back into the wilderness. I guessed he was hungry. I should have been, but my new body had freed me of that type of hunger. Instead, I just wanted to suck his cum all the time, or be covered in it. My scales absorbed it like sunshine.

We flew over so much wilderness my internal map of the Netherworld expanded by hundreds of square miles. He was looking for prey. I was looking for one of my next destinations. I wish I could have asked him where else we would find giant dragons, but I had no way to tell him where I wanted to go, not yet.

After hours of flight, I finally spotted one of the places Era had mentioned. I recognized it only because it resembled a human temple in a world of dragons, outdoors, lots of arches and columns, and I had a fading sense of reality as we passed it. I made a mental note of it as we flew by.

He landed on a... *thing*. Even now I can't tell you what it would be called. I don't think humans have ever seen one before. Some sort of giant snake with fur and deer antlers. I hoped it was an animal. I couldn't tell the difference between animal and thinking person anymore.

He devoured it while I sat and watched. At one point I rose to my feet and dared to try taking another bite. It passed straight through my jaws. I felt like a ghost when it came to eating. I can't say I missed it, but if you're not eating, what are you doing? Really, it takes up so much of our time, and everything we do leads toward it, so what would you do if you never had to eat?

All I could think to do was sit and watch. Had I been human, it would have looked disgusting, and I would have run in fear of being next. Since I was twice the size of B, and still a mound of green muscle, I watched. I wondered what he must think of me. Who was I to him? Was I this mysterious stranger who followed him around and fucked him whenever he wanted, or did he understand I used to be a person before all this, and this isn't who I really am? He knew who I used to be, but what did that make me now? I didn't know, so did he? Hell, I just enjoyed fucking around with him. I hadn't given much thought to what it meant, or what the future would be.

All of this I pondered while he ate. I missed the taste of food, but his seed had replaced the need. Yes, I craved his jizz. Even as he ate, I wanted to eat, too, and his scent had only become more potent since we had the room in the city.

I began to wonder what would happen if B wasn't in the mood. Would I starve? How long could I live without his seed? My body was made of magic, so did it even matter?

It's weird looking back on those days. Still so much I didn't understand, and my relationship with B began with sex, so it didn't seem possible it could be anything but. We were magically bound together, but we clearly enjoyed one another's scent, so was that all we needed? God Himself must have brought us together. It's as if we were made for each other, mentally and physically. I become whatever he wants, and I like whatever I become.

Oh? You want to feel these arms? Well, put your quills down and get over here. They're not just for looks.[33]

I can crush boulders even in this body.

B made my chest bigger for all of you.

Plenty of room for all of your hands.

Sometimes I cum just from people feeling me up, and I don't need time to recover. I can go again right away.

______

33 Only two surviving manuscripts contain these last few paragraphs.

SESSION 6

At this rate I'll never get to the end. Well, it's true what they say. Life is not a destination, it's a journey. We often lose sight of what that means because so many people seem to be *there*. At a place we'd all like to be, and we think that's the only possible end, so if we fail to get there, we've failed. I'll tell you what my destination used to be. When I was a hired sword, all I really wanted was enough money to buy whatever I needed from the market, and a house of my own. Not a big house. Just enough space for me. I'd spent my whole life on the move, so I wanted enough money to afford to stay still. Learn to read, learn to paint, learn to play the violin. Yes, I had an irrational desire to pick one up and learn it. I was kind of interested in pottery, so I had planned to buy a wheel and some clay and spend my days exploring. Can you imagine me doing that? An old man alone in a house making bowls? I can't see myself anywhere else than where I am now. Magic gone wrong dropped the opportunity of a lifetime at my feet. I picked it up and ran with it and I never stumbled. I think back on it now and I can see so many ways I could have wasted the opportunity. So many ways everything could have gone wrong.

You still have cum in your beard.

So where was I?

B had just finished his meal, and I took the chance to hint that I wanted to go somewhere. He seemed curious, so he let me lead. I took off and followed my internal map to that temple we had passed.

Try to imagine a desert that has lots and lots of water. Every plant we flew over had its own pond around it. I'd later learn those plants create pools of acid around themselves to survive, and the result is miles and miles of acidic lakes, each with a single tree or bush or cactus sticking out of it.

The temple sat in the middle of this. I only saw a stone slab elevated about six yards above the ground, pristine and perfect. We landed on the edge, and B bumped hips with me. He took off down the slope ahead of me, coughing flames.

In my peripheral vision, I saw people in robes looking at me, and a few were gesturing to me, but I ignored them. I had a feeling B understood why I wanted to come here, so I followed him down.

Way, way down. Strange part about that place was how soon we came to a barrier that existed on the other side but not on ours. Only two levels down, we passed through something, and I felt a muted sense of reality. I already knew what I would find, but I had to be sure.

No ramps this time. We came to a shaft, and B dove into it. My internal map put this shaft at about four thousand fathoms deep. No light whatsoever, but I could see perfectly. The further we fell, the more I felt something pulling me.

We emerged into a cavern so large it could have been a continent. Lying in the middle of this, about a fifth of the size of this cavern, lay a sleeping dragon. He had orange scales striped in yellow and red. His horns alone were large enough to crush a city. Again I had a hard time comprehending the scale of what I was seeing.

The giant's mass pulled both of us in. This time I didn't want to be scared. B dove and then leveled off just above the giant's back. We skimmed the surface. Each scale was the size of a plot of farmland. I fully expected to see clouds underneath us.

We covered enough distance for several kingdoms. Finally we came to the neck, and B banked side to side. I didn't know what this meant, but I followed him.

After flying for almost an hour, we reached the head, and B dove. We landed on the crown, in the middle of a single scale. This one scale became the horizon, and in the distance we could see gentle hills made of scales rolling up and down. The neck, the back, the wings...

I glared at B. He jumped to and fro like a puppy. I trembled at first, but then I decided to be fearless this time. I started prancing about, too. B bathed my face in fire. I opened my mouth and imitated him, and we danced on top of this scale.

The giant took several minutes to inhale, and then several more minutes to exhale. We both paused when the exhale came. The rumble it made through the air and the ground should have been audible for thousands of miles.

I wanted to ask B so many questions. I wished I could reach out to Era—I didn't want to wait for her to find me again—I had to tell her right now.

A dragon had become my *country*. This one might have been even bigger than the one at South Sect. My mind caved in on itself, and I dropped to my stomach, just in awe. B approached me and nudged my shoulder.

I lowered my head and shivered.

He wiggled his head underneath mine and raised it up. He then swiped his claws across the ground. His claws didn't even make a dent in this single scale. We were less than insects against this dragon.

B seemed gleeful here, so I rose to my feet and pranced about as well. He pranced with me, as if to say "that's the spirit."

We frolicked around on the giant's head. The giant inhaled, and then exhaled. I observed something I hadn't noticed around the other. As we danced, light began to rain down on the dragon's scales. I looked up and saw rocks suspended far, far above us. So far they hovered at the limits of my vision. Pebbles of what looked like ordinary sandstone and limestone and granite, and other rocks I couldn't name, all glowing with power. They rained magical energy onto the sleeping giant for a few minutes at a time.

I checked with B. He was looking up as well, wings fluttering. His posture said the sight was so beautiful it brought him to tears. I looked up again and counted hundreds of these suspended boulders. Some of them in the distance, over the tail, glowed and rained light down on the giant.

I felt fingers on my hind leg. B was behind me, hands sliding up my thigh. I tried to smile again and I put weight my leg so he could feel the muscles in motion. His fingers fell into every crevice. I lashed my tail. B grabbed it with his whole body. He licked it a few times. I wish I could explain how to flex tail muscles. I did it for him just to show them at work. All the dragons in town, none of them had a muscular tail, so I guessed this looked incredible even to them.

I dropped and rolled to my back, gesturing with all four legs to come closer, and B ran both hands over my stomach. The muscles lining my abdominal were deep and thick, and he appreciated every single one of them with a hand or a tongue. I craned my neck to watch him feeling me up. Took me by surprise that he wasn't out of his slit. Neither was I, come to think of it.

I held my arms out and clenched my hands. I grunted and gestured to them with my snout. B was still licking my midsection, and he looked at my arms from beneath my chest. A wave rushed through them and they doubled in thickness. I had more arm than head now. I gave each bicep a lick and then turned back to B.

B used my abdominals as a ladder to climb up and lay on my chest, muzzle to muzzle with me. Another wave, and my chest started to swell, gradually pushing him away from me. I giggled internally. I didn't want him to go away, so I reached around and cupped his rear and pressed him close to me. My chest continued bulging.

He puffed a little flame over me. I kept our muzzles together as my chest muscles grew to thrice the size of my head. I couldn't see anything but them when I looked down. It took effort to keep our snouts from separating. He loved feeling them as they swelled, and I bumped noses with him. When I let him go, my chest launched him backwards. I caught him between my thighs. He puffed more flames over my legs. I tried to laugh with him.

I don't remember what happened next. I know we didn't fuck, and he didn't make me grow any bigger. Next thing I knew we were flying, and my body was normal again. The flight out of the cave seemed to take an eternity, probably because of the pulling force the giant exerted on us. I worried we wouldn't be able to escape it and we'd be trapped on his skin forever, forced to forage whatever else fell onto it.

When we returned to the surface, I collapsed on the stone. B also dropped to his stomach next to me, wings fanned. We were both tired after a flight that long, fighting the pull of a dragon the size of a mountain.

The humans in my peripheral vision were bowing to us, reaching out and trying to stroke our scales. I felt a phantom hand on my shoulder and a few more on my tail. B seemed to enjoy their touches.

He grunted at me, gesturing at the people around us, and then aimed his snout downward, gesturing to the giant below.

I blinked, looked around.

He rolled over and invited the people to rub his belly. Nobody did, but they knelt. I noticed they had lit the torches for us. Sometimes I felt the heat.

We rested at the temple for a while. Long enough for the people to find paper and graphite. I held still while they sketched me so everyone back home could see me. When we left the temple, I had a lot on my mind, but I still made notes of the vegetation I saw along the way. I figured some of it might be familiar to someone back in Hirinda, and the map of the Netherworld would line up with the map of the "real" world somehow.

I saw lots of animals I didn't recognize. I saw bushes that actively reached out and tried to snatch these animals. The bushes seemed to be cooperating, growing new branches in one place and losing them somewhere else, trying to herd these animals to one specific location. I imagined being a human trapped in there, a hedge maze always changing and leading me to my death with dragons soaring above it all. I pondered how I hadn't seen anything else in the skies, despite many creatures possessing wings.

We didn't go home. B flew us over these bushes, then over some mountains that seemed to be covered in lava that didn't flow. Entire cliffs and hills made of liquid fire, all of it standing still. To my shock, I saw things growing down there. Trees and vine-like things, but the fire didn't burn the plants. Another nightmarish place for those who couldn't fly.

Eventually we came back to the swamp of goo. I smiled internally as I watched all the mythical animals playing down there. We flew over some new areas for me, though every area of the swamp looked the same, and the terrain was ever-changing with some parts becoming solid, others becoming goo again, branches falling in and emerging from it. I wondered what would happen if a human being fell into it.

B began a descent, but I couldn't see anything down there worth descending into. No animals around. No branches. Just more goo.

He folded his wings and picked up speed. So did I, though I really wanted to ask where we were going. The ground was coming up fast, and he seemed to want even more speed. Was this a game?

I kept my eyes on B, which prevented me from looking at the black slime rising up to meet us. I screeched at him once or twice as it came close, but B only picked up speed. I closed my eyes when we dove in. Strange. I wasn't surprised when we didn't hit solid ground. In fact, we kept going deeper into the slime. Deeper. Deeper.

I felt us pass through another magical barrier, and that's when I knew.

As soon as I thought it, we burst out of the slime and into another cavern so large I couldn't see the end of it, and on the ground, right below us, slept a giant dragoness. This one seemed smaller than the other two, but each of her scales was still large enough to build a house on top of.

Great, I thought. Now he's taking me to see them all. It's the only thing I've shown an interest in besides his slit and ass, so of course he would.

Bright red scales. All sorts of shades and tints of red.

As I expected, B took us in, and we landed on her head, near one of her horns. The scale we stood on held both of us easily. I had a difficult time imagining creatures of this size moving.

She pulled me less than the other two, and overhead I saw more suspended rocks of granite and sandstone, all glowing with power and covering her with this energy. I wondered what would happen if any of that energy hit us. In this dragon body, I felt invincible, but atop these giants, I felt as helpless as a mayfly.

All I could do was turn around in place and behold her.

B stood looking at me. He said a few things, and I tried to answer, but I only made sounds that hopefully conveyed the feeling of being awed and overwhelmed.

Moments later, I heard wings flapping overhead. I looked up, and four dragons were hovering just over us, all of them predominately blue in color.

B *skree'd* at them, but not in the sense of wanting them to go away. The dragons all slowed their flapping and dropped to an adjacent scale. That's when I caught their scents, and they all smelled similar to B.

Time to meet the family.

I sat facing them, making sure my forelegs pushed my chest out. I even tightened the muscles so they could see they were solid. B walked up to meet them, rubbed snouts with everyone. I guessed the big male was my father-in-law, the equally large female was my new mother-in-law, and the other two were B's younger brother and sister.

They were circling each other, scenting one another in various places. My eye twitched a little when the sister scented B's slit, and the father nudged his tail up and sniffed his ass. It took conscious effort to remember these were not humans. Scent meant something different to them. I couldn't even guess at the time how scent made them relate to one another.

The sounds they made were different from any other sounds I'd heard dragons make. Much more cheeping and high-pitched grunting. This would have been the first family I saw together, so I figured these were the sounds only family members made to one another.

As they mutually sniffed each other's slits and snouts and exchanged chirps and shrieks, I wondered how they found us. Had they followed us from the other temple? Why hadn't they been with B in that obsidian cave? I sat patiently and waited for some sort of signal for what I should do.

Finally the mother and father looked up from their son's slit and faced me. I gave my arms a tiny flex and took a deep breath so they could see the abs in motion.

The father approached me. I stood taller. I had twice as much bulk, but I still felt intimidated. To my surprise, he lowered his head and stuck his nose in my slit.

The rest of the family followed, and in a moment I had four dragon noses scenting between my legs. I checked with B, and he sat down, watching. He seemed nervous, too. This wasn't unwelcome, but it was a shock.

Then I felt tongues.

I had no idea how dragon society worked, so I sat there and let them inspect their eldest son's new husband.

With four tongues inside my slit, of course I came out, and they sniffed the shaft as it grew up my stomach. No tongues on my dick, but lots of sniffing. They followed the tip as it rose. I wondered how big B would make it. It stopped growing when it slid between my pecs. Larger than normal, but not unbelievable either. B still wanted to show me off.

The mother looked up at me and nuzzled my snout. I nuzzled her back. B said a few things. She replied over her shoulder. Next thing I knew, I had four snouts nuzzling mine, so I returned the gesture.

Then the moment I had been waiting for. All four sat in front of me, and I took that as my cue to inspect them in return. I rose to all fours, dick still hard and jutting out between all four of my legs, and walked to the father. I hoped dragons didn't have some sort of etiquette of order, so I simply went right to left.

B's father smelled like B, but had his own variety. At this point I felt licking his slit and sniffing his dick would be a breach of protocol, and not doing this would also be a breach. I decided to err on the side of caution and just scented him.

Then I moved to B's mother. The woman's scent was fascinatingly different. It was as if it had been designed to be stimulating to males, like flowers were to bees. It didn't do anything to me, and I was glad, since this was my in-law, but I could tell how the two scents fit together. That's a good way to describe it. Even I could tell they fit together.

B's two other siblings were younger, but now I knew their scents, too. I hoped they didn't mind my dick still being out. It wouldn't shrink back into my slit for some reason, and it wouldn't stop dripping.

I was starting to figure out what the appeal was. It looked weird to human eyes, but there really was a lot of information from doing this. The slit was where they had identity. That's where their scent came from. Sniffing their ass was actually more intimate—that's where information on health was. Yeah, try to imagine how knowing all of this about a person with just a casual sniff would change how things work between people. I was just beginning to see.

Meanwhile, the giant inhaled.

And then exhaled.

Inhaled.

Exhaled.

I expected B to make my muscles grow, or suddenly stretch my dick to poke someone in the snout, but he seemed to be actively hiding this. He had hidden it from the Judges, from other dragons around town, and now his own family.

Now I had their scents, and it was like I had always known them. I stood before them, looking at his parents and siblings, willing my dick to shrink and stop dripping. B wanted it out, and he wanted it to leak in front of them. I couldn't tell if they were impressed or not.

Finally the mother rose to all fours and made a high-pitched cheep to me.

I guessed it meant "son."

I didn't know the appropriate response, so I repeated the sound.

The father said it, too.

The two younger dragons said something else, but still in a familiar tone.

We all nuzzled. The mother scented my dick again. So did the father, this time licking it, but only once. I stood still, thrilled to be part of the family. I had met the parents or siblings of several women I had been with over the years. Several of the men, too. Never had I been honored with the familiar.[34]

Then B stood against me and rubbed flanks. I rubbed him back, and B walked in front of me, tail up, and his scent hit me. It was so strong I think I could have cum just from

---

34 That is, the familiar voice, or the informal. In M's time, the language used the formal (*you*) in all situations except family relations. In the original sources, M addresses Era and the scribes with the informal (*thou*) at times, which would have been a meaningful gesture in the 800s. The majority of surviving documents have been altered to use the informal only to refer to members of lesser social class, as was the law from the 1100s through the 1700s, a deliberate attempt by the monarchies to embed social stratification into the language itself. This edition uses the formal exclusively.

that. He looked back at me, breathing and grunting as if I had already mounted him.

I checked with his family. They stood around us, waiting. I wished I could laugh.

I climbed up B's back, wrapped my arms around his torso, pressed my pecs against his shoulders, and flexed all the muscles in my legs as I shoved my dick under his tail. My hips touched his. He had taken the whole thing, and I felt my legs tingle as he made it grow inside of him.

I kept my thrusts deep, and I squeezed him around his torso as hard as I could. I stretched my wings, showing those muscular things as well. I wanted them to see every muscle at work fucking their son and brother on top of that giant.

As I sped up, I pushed his front half into the... ground and pinned him. He could not move, and I rammed him deep and hard. His family watched impassively. I expected to see a couple of dicks come out, but none did. I would later learn dragons are not stimulated by the sight of sex, but rather the smell. That's why they stood where they did. They couldn't smell what we were doing. It's respectful. Watching two dragons fuck is proof they are together. Nobody has to say it or declare it. In their culture, that's how they know. His family was just witnessing our marriage. That's all it was to them.

B blew his load on the giant dragon's head. When I smelled it, it made my hips tingle, and I shot one of my own into him.

I pulled out, and my dick was still pulsing, leaving an even bigger trail of jizz around. He rubbed snouts with his family one by one, and they rubbed snouts with me even as my dick leaked.

Apparently this satisfied them. I felt a bit swollen with pride having impressed my in-laws. Finally, family members I got along with, and they even gave me the familiar. But... what had B told them about me? How did he explain why I couldn't speak? All I seemed to know how to do was grunt and fuck their son. Was that enough in a dragon marriage?

As a family, we took flight and sped out of the cavern. We picked up enough speed to burst through the magical barrier again and cut through the swamp. B's family flew off in the direction of the city. B and I stood on a partially solid piece of goo and watched them go. Finally my dick had gone back into my slit, and that helped me stand at ease.

When they were out of sight, B nuzzled me and pranced with his hind legs. I gave him some familiar-sounding, high-pitched growls in return.

My groin tingled and suddenly my muscles doubled in size. He nuzzled my shoulder and then my pecs. They swelled independently of the rest of me, and now he nudged me over, and I rolled to my back in the goo, which felt like a bed of straw. He climbed on top of me, felt my chest, licked it, ran his claws down the muscles.

Now I reached up and felt his arms. Compared to me, he seemed so small. Not frail, just... normal. Yes, he had the same build as his siblings. He had muscles under his scales, but not nearly like mine.

As I felt him, my hand grew, and now his hand fit in the palm of mine. I held his hand as another wave stretched me out, and now I looked down on him, sitting on my stomach, tracing the lines in my shoulders and neck. His dick had slipped out again.

I tried to tell him you're welcome.

I stretched out again, and my height rose. My arms were almost as thick as his whole body now. I could barely see over my chest to look at him.

I had the feeling B had been holding back for a long time, and now he released his hold on me. I felt like a bucket collecting rainwater. Just getting higher and higher, deeper and deeper, one wave after another, so many they blended together, and I just lay on my back and let it happen.

B had perched himself on my stomach, watching me become his country.

I know I slipped out of my slit again, and I had the feeling my dick arched over him, probably dripping on him.

I could barely see myself stretching out. I lay in the goo only up to my stomach. I rested on the bottom. My arms were so bulky I don't think I could have walked. My chest muscles stuck so far in front of me I couldn't see down my own torso no matter how I moved my neck. I couldn't move my neck side to side it was so thick. I did manage to get a look at my legs, and my thighs rubbed together from hip to knee no matter how far apart I spread them. My dick had to squeeze between them, and it was as thick as my arm.

None of the humans I had been with had ever thanked me so generously for impressing their families.

The tops of the trees must have been a hundred meters down. I felt B on my stomach. One of my abdominal muscles had become his perch. I wished I could see him, but this felt so good I didn't dare try to move him.

My height rose another yard with the next wave, and then another hit just behind it, and I swelled another couple yards.

I lifted my arms and checked the muscles. Bigger than my head, and the scales gave way to veins thicker than my fingers underneath. The veins spread over the rest of my body, and now I had little mountains of them running across my chest, what of them I could see.

I roared as six waves hit me one after the other, and my neck thickened and legs stretched and bowled over a few solid branches of swamp slime.

My dick slipped between my pecs and kissed me on the snout.

I felt dragon semen hitting my stomach. My scales absorbed it. Again, I felt more together.

And then I saw a robed shadow standing on the end of my nose.

"Oh God, Era, not now!"

"Pardon?"

"I wish you could see me now."

I had a hard time forming coherent thoughts as my body expanded and the swamp became smaller and smaller.

"It wasn't hard to find you this time. What's happening?"

"The giant dragons! They're... I found two more! B led me to them! The second one was even bigger than the first!"

"I just received word from Lowerik. They sent me a few sketches they made of the two of you. If you don't mind me saying so, you are a lovely couple."

All I could do was pant for a moment as the clouds came a bit closer. Was B testing my limit? Did seeing the giant dragons turn him on and now he felt free indulge himself?

"It's hard for me to talk like this. B is making me grow right now. I'm getting huge. He likes his men big."

"I can tell from the sketch. I never will understand men, especially queers."

"Their city. I think it's held together by magic. Their magic. I mean... they have pieces of granite and marble over their buildings. They do something to the bones, but I can't tell what. The giant dragons have our rocks hovering over them, sending energy over them. And I met my in-laws."

She chuckled and said, "My condolences, and thank you for confirming materials in our world have magical properties in theirs. Now we know those giant dragons are there deliberately, and their presence weakens the barrier between our world and the Netherworld."

I barely understood her. My dick had forced its way into my mouth, and I was sucking on it. My neck grew, my height shot up, and the dick fell short of my muzzle. My pecs inflated, and I lost even more of my vision. Apparently B wanted to look up a solid wall of muscle. It felt so good I blew a load on my face. It passed straight through the robed figure on my snout. My dick did not go soft. In fact, it thickened, pushing my pecs apart.

"Any new information on dragons?"

"Plenty, but none of it makes sense." I strained to think straight as I expanded again. "They seem to be sharing tiny rocks from our world. Tiny magical rocks. Not buying. Just trading. They don't seem to have money."

As I thought this, B flew off my stomach and hovered in front of me. He hit me with a blast of fire and then landed on my chest to one side of my cock. I nudged him with my nose, making family sounds, hoping to tell him I enjoyed this.

With him off my stomach, I sat up straight. Wasn't comfortable with four legs, but at least now I could see my legs, and they were the size of a small town. My dick could have been a bridge between two sides of a forest canyon. I noticed my head had almost reached the clouds. B lay down, feeling my chest. I flexed it for him.

"You said you went to a third place. Do you know which?"

"It's under this swamp I told you about before. I don't know where it is."

"I haven't heard from any of the other places yet, but now we have three confirmed giants. B took you there, so dragons in general know about them. What's happening?"

My dick hit the clouds before my head did. I strained to lean over my pecs and see the rest of me. B noticed what I wanted to do and grew my neck up so I could see.

My claws had grown to ridiculous proportions. So had my feet. I had at least fifty abdominal muscles around my stomach, and my chest looked like kingdoms by themselves. I had no sense of scale anymore.

"Concentration of natomic energy is enormous," Era said. "Are you all right?"

"Is... Is there an upper limit to this?"

"We're not certain. That weapon was experimental."

"My head is in the clouds."

"Why would he want you to be that size?"

"He likes big men. His family likes me, and B is thanking me for making a good impression. I think."

I waved some clouds out of my way, making them break up. I think I had approached the point where someone could have built a house on one of my scales.

"Michael, this feels strange. The concentration of natomic mass is forming a well. I may have to back out or I will be pulled into—"

Something cracked. Not like an earthquake, but reality itself. Not even reality—something underneath reality shattered. All around me the swamp flickered. I could see trees. Human trees. I mean, trees in the normal world. A farm. A house. Several houses around me. The swamp and the trees existed at the same time on top of one another.

B noticed it too, for he turned around on my chest and peered over it.

Moments later, the farmland settled into the swamp, and the cracking sensation ceased. A couple dozen people were down there, some with harvesting sickles and baskets. They now floated in an ocean of black slime, and trees were half submerged in it.

The people began to melt. Their skin became the slime. They screamed as the trees that had come with them became twisted and thorny.

Era disappeared.[35]

All right, all right, I know I've been growing. Good place to stop.

That's right. Sit on my lap.

I bite you and you get hard? I should have been a scribe.

You really like my legs, don't you? They're thicker than your whole body.

See, I can lift four of you. Two in each arm. Not even straining.

Where did you get metal poles this thick? Did you have them made just for me?

There. That's one bent in half.

Here's a metal pretzel for you. Yes, you may feel the arms that made it. I'm pretty swollen now from all that effort. Took B a while to figure out how to make that happen. Usually he leaves them swollen all the time, but it looks better when they relax. Helps some humans feel more comfortable around me.

B likes the muscular tail. I've heard lots of humans say it looks disgusting, but they're just jealous. He'd give me wings in this body, too, if he could. I'm the one who suggested leaving them off. You want to see?

Oh, you like watching me sprout wings. Just wait.

---

35 Only one surviving manuscript contains the following paragraphs at the end of Session 6. This original source was discovered in the year 1198, under the pillow of King Nitae III, mere hours after he passed away in his sleep.

Yes, this feels just as good as it looks.

B has never made them this thick before. I don't think I can fly. Nope. When I have a proper dragon body, I can use them.

You like watching the wings? Come closer so you can see them in motion.

Strange, isn't it, feeling muscles that don't exist on a human body?

Forget what they say. Fine art is meant to be touched. You can feel me any time you want. B adds new details every day. It's what he does when he's daydreaming. He still thinks of muscular bodies a lot. He never outgrew that. In fact, I think he does even more than when he was younger.

Sometimes I like looking at myself in a mirror just to find what he's changed.

We used to coordinate. We knew exaggerating some areas instead of others would make this nobleman uncomfortable, or that other monarch. Was a great source of joy for forty years, keeping them on edge, showing them that they are not the highest. That there exists someone else they have to tolerate. They can't sit on their asses and expect other people to cater to their whims. That's what I wanted to tell them all these years. That they're not as important as they think they are. Nobody needs them, but they need the people, and I never let them forget that.

Keep your hands on my rear. He's indulging you now. It's fun feeling him change me like this.

SESSION 7

Who's been talking to B?

All of you, I see.

B doesn't usually grant requests,[36] so you must have amused him. My balls are the size of watermelons. I haven't had balls in as long as I can remember. They have heft. Are you trying to make me suffer? I can barely move with these things. Well, I'm glad you're amused. I'm more curious how you talked to B without me knowing.

So, picking up from yesterday, I don't remember exactly what happened immediately after. The next thing I knew, we were back in the bone tower, and I was normal sized. Well, normal for me. B was just staring out the window, not really looking at anything. So did I. I didn't even know how long it had been.

It seemed clear by now that we had been the only witnesses in the Netherworld to the event. We watched dragons. I noticed the tower had rotated while we had been gone, so now we had a view of the entire city. Seems dragons did have a marketplace, but not for food or wares or anything. Nobody in the dragon city seemed to make anything. Instead they compared and traded rocks. Not gems, not pieces of bone. Ordinary rocks, from the human side. I wondered if dragons didn't have daily markets, but only met like this once a week or something.

---

36 *We drew dicks and other obscene images, and B rendered them on M's scales for us, all over his body. I'm pleased B took our suggestions.*

I watched, still trying to make sense of everything.

Era reappeared in the air just beyond the window. I glanced at B, but he didn't react.

"We're receiving reports that several farms in the kingdom of Wentinworth are covered in black slime. People are missing."

"Wentinworth," I said, mentally. "So the swamp is way out in the middle of nowhere."

"Time and distance are apparently not a one-to-one ratio between the atomic world and the natomic. Do you have any idea how large you grew?"

"Big enough for my head to be in the clouds."

"The region is safe to be in now. Apparently whatever happened is no longer occurring. I take it you are back to normal size?"

"B and I are in the city again. We're both just staring at the townspeople right now. I'm back to my usual size. We both have been in a fog for a while. He's just as shaken by what happened as I am. I'm sorry."

"Nobody blames you, Michael, but the monarchs are beginning to wonder what's happening. I've heard whispers of the other eight kingdoms becoming suspicious of Queen Unari's activities."

"They have every reason to be worried."

"We'll likely have to involve them anyway. Do you have time to talk?"

"I think so. Those people... They became something else when they came over. They changed into other things. I mean, they were still human, but they seemed distorted. Feral. Nothing left to save."

"I'll address that in a moment," she answered. "First, this confirms a new theory we arrived at only recently. One of the ideas revealed to us in the new calculations as opposed to the old style of magic being done by intuition.

Atoms exert force when enough of them are collected together. Gather enough of the same type in one place, and it will pull other objects closer. Natoms have this same property. Dragons appear to be different. This brings me to the giants. Collect enough of their natoms in one place, and they begin to pull *atoms* closer. The math implies they could bend reality far enough to break. The result is the weakening of the barrier between our two worlds."

"I follow you so far."

"Our calculations indicate your *increased* presence combined with the nearby giant bent reality enough to force the two particles to coexist and interact. It likely forced natoms to combine with atoms, and the result was what you described happened to the people."

"Shit."

"We are still running the numbers, but with three giants identified, and the other sites presumed to have them as well, it seems likely these giants are positioned evenly across the whole land. It is exactly what one would do if the intent was[37] to break the barrier across all nine kingdoms at once."

"Shit."

"I won't speculate on the reason. I don't know enough about dragons or their mages to say. But when the delegates of the nine kingdoms meet, we will have to present this information, and I can predict the conclusion they will draw from it."

"Shit."

"Do you have any insights yet as to why they would create giant dragons? We've already concluded the purpose is to break the barrier, but without knowing more about their society, we don't know why."

---

[37] Some original sources use *were.*

"None of these giants are in populated areas, are they?"

"So far, no."

"Then it doesn't make sense for this to be an invasion. If I wanted to overthrow nine kingdoms in one motion, I'd have a giant dragon under every castle keep. Why make an army fly for days just to reach the monarchs?"

"I agree there are too many unknowns. The conference has not happened yet, but time passes faster here than where you are. Distance is also compressed where you are relative to here, from what I figure. It implies natoms are more dense than atoms, which is likely why they do not normally interact."

"Huh?"

"Sorry. I'm tired. Focus on dragon society. Try to find out what's going on. If possible, find their leaders. Those Judges you mentioned. And by all means, try to figure out how to talk to them."

"Working on it. This isn't easy. I've figured out they use different pitches for different situations. They use high pitches for family and friends. Low tones for everyone else."

"Formal and informal, which implies a social hierarchy. We may yet have much in common."

"Era, there's something I have to know."

She looked up at me. She still had no face, but somehow I saw concern in her eyes. "Anything."

"If I did come back, and if you did manage to put me back in a body, what are the odds I won't be put on trial for the deaths of those farmers and setting off a war between you and the Netherworld?"

The robed figure standing on the air in front of the window didn't move or speak for a while.

"Queen Unari does not hold you responsible for what has happened, but I can't speak for the other monarchs."

"It's not just monarchs I have to worry about. Aristocrats are incredibly touchy. If you so much as look at them wrong—if they feel you didn't grovel enough in their presence or show them enough respect, they'll have you executed. I know. I saw it a few times."

"It's too soon for me to say, Michael. When we present our work to the delegates, I promise we will speak of you as a spy delivering valuable information to us about a rival nation."

"Thanks."

"It's the truth. I worry for the future of Queen Unari. Now that arcane research is affecting other kingdoms, she may have to fight to retain her throne. Our research may have to switch to warfare, which is something I do not want."

"I want to go back to exploring. This was fun then. Why does everything have to end up being war?"

"War is good for the ruling families."

"They make money, and they gain status when the dust settles. Research into the arcane arts was good for me. I was this close to being rich, and nobody had to die."

She laughed. "If things were that simple. You said you met your in-laws?"

"I think B was trying to keep us from meeting, but they found us on one of those giants. Was weird. I had to sniff everyone's crotch."

She chuckled. "I see."

"And then B and I ended up fucking on top of that giant, in front of them. They were sniffing us and licking us after, and nobody thought it was weird."

"And I thought meeting *my* in-laws was awkward."

"This wasn't awkward at all. Weird, but... I know them now. They like my scent, and I like theirs, so it feels like... we're family. That was fun in a way."

"Fun after meeting the family. Wish mine had been. My late husband's family ignored me. When they did speak to me, they treated me like a child. The men expected me to serve them beer all the time, and they never even looked at me."

"I'm sorry. I've met men who talked to their wives that way. What did your family think of that?"

"My husband's family had land. I knew going in that's the only reason my parents wanted me to marry him. My parents had livestock and not much else. They had to pay tribute to the landlord to keep their animals on it, on top of what they had to pay to the lord who owned everyone's land. Our marriage meant my parents wouldn't have to pay rent anymore. If my husband treated me like manure under a horse's hoof, it was worth it to them."

"Marriage is politics. I avoided both until now."

"Funny. I inquired about my family a few years ago. The marriage agreement wasn't annulled. My parents still own the land. They're better off than ever without rent hanging over their heads."

"Do you ever plan to visit?"

"Never, but I don't blame my parents for using me the way they did. It's what families do when they see a chance to improve their lot in life. It brings me a little prickle of joy to hear your in-laws watched you in bed. This social custom sounds refreshing."

"I have a lot to learn about how their society works. I'm glad you got away from that place."

"So am I. I'll contact you after the conference. Take care of yourself."

"Good luck, Era."

She faded into the air. I turned to B. He was staring at me. He gestured with his hand out the window, and then to me.

My neck curled back in what I hoped he would interpret as surprise. Did he know? Had he seen her? Could he hear us?

That's when B pointed to his horn, tilting his head toward me. A tiny piece of limestone rested in a cavity designed to hold such a pebble. That rock had not been there before, so he had just recently acquired it. Now I had a flood of questions. When did he get that? What did it do? Why hadn't he had one before? And why did dragons seem to have a couple cavities in their horns made specifically for these rocks, but the Judges had them embedded into their scales?

B began talking. I listened. I would have sold my soul to the Devil right then if it meant I could understand the dragon language. I had a feeling B had all the answers, and for all I knew he was telling me these answers right now, but they all flew by me like seeds in the wind.

He got up and glided from our little alcove. I joined him in the "market" among a hundred other dragons, all grunting and chirping and eeping. Some were comparing rocks in their horns, and I saw a few of them glow with energy. One rock did not glow at all, but when she gave that rock to someone else, that person glowed with power.

B and I were surrounded, and then he spoke in a tone that made everyone stop what they were doing and turn to face us. I felt on the spot, but I stood like royalty and made sure they could see my muscles bunching up in this posture. We had a crowd. An audience. I prepared myself for whatever B wanted to do.

To my surprise, he did not make me grow. Instead, as he spoke, other people began removing the rocks from their horns and passing them to B. My blue dragon inserted them into his skull and said a few things to me. When I failed to respond, he handed that rock back to the person and took someone else's from their hand.

We became the marketplace. I didn't know what to do, so I sat down and let B do all the talking. I think every person in the city let B borrow their rock, and every time he gave it back. Some of them tried to find a place on me to insert a rock, and after a subtle wave that added a cavity to my horn, they tried putting them in me. None of them seemed to do anything, and I felt no different with a rock in me verses no rock.

Dragons touched me. They talked to me. I got the sensation they were trying to reach me. I wanted to reply, but I feared sounding stupid if I tried.

By now, the sun had come up. B had had a hundred different rocks in him, and nothing seemed to make a difference. I noticed nothing unusual after about that many rocks in my horn.

I felt lots of hands on me. I didn't get the feeling they were groping. B now lacked any sort of stone in his horns.

I noticed B's scent seemed more potent than before. It went to my groin, and it brought my nose between his legs. I sniffed and licked his slit. I was enticing him to come out, and I licked his entire length right there in the public square before I realized what I was doing. Funny. Their word for that area is *bonespace*, but that's not a good translation.

He rolled to his back, and I stood over him, my dick resting on his stomach, covering much of it. He didn't seem worried about doing this in public, so neither would I, and the marketplace just moved around us.

B lay sprawled out on his back, wings fanned underneath him. He held my dick with his hind feet, and held my arms with his fore. I bucked my hips and shoved my cock in, savoring the first brush of my barbs against him. He wrapped his hind legs around my hips. I bucked him a few times, and he felt my arms. I made sure to flex for him.

I felt noses and tongues sniffing underneath me. A few people had broken away from demonstrating and exchanging tiny rocks to sniff and lick us. I felt a little weird doing this in the open, but I never went soft. B's scent kept me out of my slit at all times. He would later tell me those dragons weren't getting a thrill out of smelling us; they were tasting our bond. Just information to them. Some of them would later tell me we smelled like the perfect couple.

My cock swelled while inside him, and B gasped and rolled his head back, showing me his throat. My arms also grew a little, not enough to make me look bigger, but certainly enough for him to feel as he braced himself against me. I think the cuts between them deepened, and I felt the muscles in my neck doing the same thing. Barely enough to notice, but he must have.

I smelled him close to finishing, so I rose higher and angled my neck so I could suck him. His jizz tasted like cider. I wondered about that even in the moment as I gulped it all down, feeling more solid and real inside this body with every drop. He felt my neck the whole time I ate.

I didn't even need to speed up or fuck him harder. My hips tingled on their own, and I released. I felt multiple noses and tongues sniffing and licking at our hips. I raised a leg so some of them could get a better view, and more muzzles moved in.

Meanwhile people around us exchanged rocks and grunted and mumbled amongst themselves. I pulled out and stood over him, dick on his chest, still pulsing and leaking. The tongues and muzzles sniffed at it as well. I looked around and realized just how big I was compared to the others. Some stood taller than me, but I had the thickest arms and largest chest. Nobody but me had a rippling neck or tail either. Everyone else looked so normal.

B lay back and gasped. He rolled over, and I climbed off him, taking a small group of muzzles sniffing and licking with me. My dick touched the ground, and those muzzles followed it as it retreated back into my slit.

B had seen someone approaching. I recognized her as one of the Judges. The stones embedded in her scales all glowed. I felt the need to kneel, but I couldn't do that easily on four legs, so I crouched to be lower than her.

B approached her as if he had not just had a cock in him a minute before the queen showed up. He touched snouts with her and then turned to me. I should have taken the hint that I didn't need to act like I was in the presence of royalty, but I couldn't shake the feeling. I rose a little, but I still kept a low stance. By now my dick had finally retreated back into my body, and the group of sniffing muzzles separated from me and melted back into the crowd of winged lizards trading pretty rocks. I noticed one dragon who had a piece of red-colored rock glowed white while it was in his horn, and the person he gave it to glowed green.

B and this Judge—mage, queen, whoever—stood and talked. I had a feeling they were talking about me.

To my left, a dragon removed a tiny rock from her horn and passed it to another in front of her. He inserted the rock. Nothing happened, so he gave it back. When she put it back into her horn, nothing seemed to happen with her either. Moments later, she gave it to someone else, and this person's horn began to shimmer. He gave her the rock that had been in his horn, and now her scales seemed to glow. They parted ways, but they remained in the marketplace hustle. To my surprise, both of them tried to trade these rocks with others, but the reaction they got did not seem to be favorable, so they ended up keeping the stones.

I looked at B and the Judge. They were still talking. B looked at me from time to time. I wish I had known what to say. I touched snouts with him a couple times if only to show I was listening. Nobody but me seemed to consider this Judge a reason to bend a knee, but after all my years watching what happened to people who misbehaved in the presence of the nobility, I didn't want to risk standing all the way up. The strain made the muscles in my legs and shoulders bulge obscenely. They were pushing my chest out even further. I could have crushed a brick between them I was working so hard to be lower than this person.

She said a few things and then swiped her hand in front of herself. A phantom object appeared: a brass candlestick.

I straightened up and approached it. I sniffed it, and surprisingly it had a scent. That must be what pure brass smelled like. I looked at B and made a few cheeping sounds in the familiar tone.

B and the Judge both looked at me, and then they faced one another and continued talking. I watched the image as it rotated. It didn't look like a real candlestick, rather someone's memory of what a candlestick should be. After a moment, it flickered out of existence, and I faced the Judge. I made more familiar sounds.

B hung his head. The Judge turned and walked away. She waved her neck and slipped into the air and out of sight.

As soon as she was gone, B grunted at me and took off running through the marketplace. I followed, wondering why weren't taking flight. He waited until we had left the market square before spreading his wings and leading us out of the city.

Not a casual flight. He picked up so much speed I struggled to keep up. The map in my head told me he seemed to be heading to the cave where I had shown him my hand print, and sure enough, that's exactly where he took me.

Now he led me through the cave system, and at the border between our two worlds, where the world turned dim, he stopped and looked at me.

He drew a simple candlestick in the stone with his claw, and then looked out into the cave.

I remembered how far it was to the other side, and I remembered how long I would have to walk to reach civilization. I did not think the binding spell would allow us to be that far apart. I also remembered the entrance to this place was too small for me to fit as a dragon.

That's when it hit me. If there were places where dragons could enter our world, he would have taken me there. What if there were no places for full-size dragons to enter the world made of atoms?

I understood what he wanted me to do, but I doubted I could find anything. I drew a candle and a little flame in the holder, hoping to show him I knew what he wanted.

He licked my muzzle, and then I changed back into a human. A naked, cold, and scared human being. After being huge for so long, suddenly being the size of one of B's fingers made me feel like a kitten. No time to lose. I ran through the barrier between worlds. The normal world, the one of atoms, still looked dim and foreboding to me. Without pausing to look back, I ran into the narrow stone corridor. It seemed to be a solid wall of debris, but I remembered the way through it.

The chamber on the other side held empty bowls and glass bottles. People had once made potions and other enchantments here. All of it had long since rotted away. No shortage of candle sticks here, but they were iron or tin. Everything of value had been looted centuries ago, so I didn't waste my time searching the place.

I began walking up the stairs to what likely would have been the living quarters for these people. As I did, I felt short of breath, and the invisible rope tightened.

The beds had been made of straw, and they had all decayed to dust. Most of the wood in here had rotted into mud. What little remained had mushrooms growing on it. Nothing else here but fragments of pottery and glass.

I heard snarling noises. Claws clicking. I peeked around the corner and saw a fenrir sniffing about.

Now I won't bore you with the details here, as it's not that important. B heard me shouting and he took the hint and grew my muscles to such ridiculous proportions I could barely move. The fenrir couldn't bite through all the muscle, and I didn't bleed. I tore the wolf in half with my bare hands, but I'm sure you don't want me to waste time describing that in vivid detail.[38]

After I killed that fenrir, I smelled something.

Brass.

I let my nose guide me to a pile of grunge, and I clawed it with my bare hands. I noticed my hands had scales again, and claws had appeared. B was having a difficult time keeping me in human form. I continued scratching at it, and then I pulled up a doorknob.

I sniffed around for other hints of brass, and I found a few coins that had been buried under piles of mushrooms. Probably not pure brass, but they might be useful. Three coins total. I carried them with the doorknob back down the stone steps.

I could barely breathe. The rope didn't feel too tight, and I knew I had gone more than fifty yards away from B. I

---

38 *Amusing to think that was B's first instinct to help M defend himself.*

wondered if he had control over how far away I could be. I ran back down the stone floor, noticing my legs had scales, too. In fact, at some point my skin had taken leave, and now I had green scales covering me. My muzzle grew back as I made my way back through the collapsed hallway. I became a two-legged dragon carrying a doorknob and a few worthless coins.

The further in I went, the more relief I felt. I hoped B sensed I was on my way back, and that he could smell I had found something.

When I emerged, I saw B lying on his stomach, clutching his head in agony. I ran up to him, finally breathing normally, and his headache seemed to lift. As I crossed the barrier, I doubled over and fell on my hands. I couldn't walk anymore, and my body started to fill out. B had let go, and now I swelled into the muscled dragon I had grown accustomed to.

As I did, B inspected what I had brought back. At first he looked forlorn, but then he brightened as he scented the objects.[39] As my neck stretched and my thighs thickened, I wanted to tell him how lucky we were that he had left my sense of smell intact, and that someone had made doorknobs and coins out of brass, and that these things just happened to have been under decaying piles of wood, where nobody had disturbed them in centuries.

We left in a hurry. The doorknob felt so tiny in my hand, and the coins practically disappeared into the folds of my scales. I clutched them for my life as we flew back to the city.

Yes, they are as heavy as they look. Try to lift them.

Don't hurt yourself.

---

39 *M stood up and began walking. His testicles are bouncing against his thighs. His cock hangs past his knees. The veins on it are as thick as my wrist.*

That's it, keep trying to get out from under them. It only excites me. Feels good, you wiggling around down there.

Who requested B give me a human cock?

Someone's getting this, and if my nose is right, it's you. The innocent one. You're not innocent, are you? Come here.[40]

---

40 *He growled at me. I had never been so enticed in my life. He invited me to feel his legs. I studied them. His muscles guided me up to his stomach and chest, and then to his arms. Finally I reached his face. His breath smelled beautiful. I needed more. He gave me more of his scent that day.*

SESSION 8

Oh no.
All nine of you? Show me.
Scales all over your arms.
You're growing a tail.
Your legs. Is that a slit? Another penis inside it?
I didn't know this could happen. None of the mages or Judges raised the possibility. Well, maybe this is what happens when you suck down too much dragon seed.

It's normally not possible for dragons and humans to fuck around, and I'm not a true dragon, so who knows what this is doing to you. We should stop playing around and get to the end. Wouldn't want all of you to become too disfigured. You might be hanged as demons or something.[41]

Let's try to speed this up. I only found out what they were doing long after the fact. We visited that Judge again and gave her the brass. She seemed impressed we had some already. They had only seen brass before as candlesticks, so they didn't realize other things had been made out of it.

She took us to some bone building that had all sorts of magical objects in it, and by magical I mean perfectly ordinary. Knives, nails, pieces of wood, flasks of what looked

---

41 This is one of many passages scrubbed from public records after the failed revolution of 924. Any copies discovered to contain mention of humans acquiring dragon traits were burned on order of the Scribe's Guild. Despite this, rumors about the Guild circulated for centuries until the printing press spread literacy to more people, and the Guild adapted, becoming an alliance of book publishers.

like urine and blood. It looked like a barn somewhere out in the countryside. Really, it did.

She melted the brass and separated all the other metals from it, and I swear I saw stars in it. Now with a pot of pure brass, she crafted two stones and did some sort of ritual. I saw phantoms flying about us the whole time. Distorted figures of humans and animals.

She then put one of the stones in my horn, and the other in B's.

Nothing.

They looked just as disappointed as I felt. I deduced this was a last ditch effort to communicate with me, as they both directed words at me several times, and then paused, as if expecting me to answer. When I didn't, her posture changed, and she began yelling at B.

B tried to leave, but she did something and encased us in some sort of energy curtain. The room disappeared. So did the floor. Stars replaced everything. Somehow we were standing on what looked like the night sky, and I had a feeling nobody could hear the Judge as she screamed at B.

I moved between them and tried to calm things down. Impulse to appease aristocrats, remember. With a flick of her hand she moved me aside and addressed B again. Now B stood low and shivered. He looked at me. I tilted my head, wanting to help but not sure how I could.

My legs tingled, and a growth spurt washed through me. My height rose about half a yard, and my arms and shoulders swelled. My leg muscles also swelled, squishing against each other.

The Judge looked from B to me and then back to B.

Another spurt rushed through me, and my height rose another yard. I spread my legs to adjust for my new height and length, and now I towered over both of them, barely able to see over my chest.

My claws shot forward, and my horns curled in front of me like vines. In a few seconds, my claws were half as long as my arm.

The Judge turned to B and told him something.

My claws then retracted, and my horn uncurled and returned to normal as well. The brass egg she had made for me fell out and bounced off the inky floor.

My scales changed from green to black, the new color washing over me like the tide.

Then I noticed starry patterns on my scales. I must have blended in perfectly with the little reality she had created.

She dropped the canvas, and we stood in the room full of magical objects again. I filled it. I looked at B. He was still low and cowering. I leaned down and bumped his leg with my nose. It didn't seem to help him.

Our secret was out. Now what?

All the Judges walked out of the air and joined us inside. They were using some sort of magic to make the room bigger, because they should not have been able to fit.

The room faded to yellow, everything dropped away, and B and I found ourselves in court again, and this time my bulk took up most of our platform. I met the eyes of every Judge. I wanted to tell them their jewelry was fake.

The Judges growled and mumbled in turn. B sometimes answered. Their tone remained formal, and if I read their mannerisms right, they went from terrified to merely concerned.

Minutes later, the Judges, or mages, rose as one and backed away, vanishing into the air, leaving me and B on this platform over the ocean. I dropped to my stomach and rolled to my side. B slipped under my arm and lay against me. I didn't grow this time. I must have been big enough.

I wondered why we didn't just fly off, but I had no map of this place, and I guessed B had none either. There could be no land for thousands of miles, and how long could a dragon fly? What would happen if a dragon became tired over the ocean? Did this place even exist, or did the dragon mages create it just for this kind of thing?

I figured B finally had to come clean about what I was, and the mages did not like it. Not only had we accidentally broken the barrier between the worlds, their magic didn't seem to affect me. Sure, I'd want someone like that in a jail, too.

We waited for a while. I didn't turn to vapor. Had I been human, I would have wanted to sleep because I was bored.

Moments later, I saw the shadowy figure of Era standing just in front of me.

"I bring grave news."

"I'm ready."

"Representatives of the nine kingdoms met, and they do not like what they see."

"They met already?"

"It has been three weeks since we last spoke. We used some of our new magic techniques to allow them to communicate over distances instantly. It took all this time for the deliveries to arrive. We wanted to show them that the research Queen Unari is doing is benign and beneficial to all. It might've helped but not enough to outweigh the rest."

"Shit."

"The nine kingdoms are afraid of what you've found in the Netherworld. They are convinced the only possible reason to do this is to collapse the barrier and allow dragons to invade our world. With that much natomic mass, it will force natoms to replace atoms, and we will all become part of the Netherworld."

"I don't think that's what's happening."

"I have to admit, it's convincing, but I emphasized our spy has only been there for a few months, and we need more information. Have you learned anything else?"

"B doesn't seem to think of the Judges as royalty. Today we went to the marketplace, but everyone just traded pieces of sandstone and limestone. I think they were trying to find something that would allow them to talk to me. Their magic doesn't seem to work on me, and the judges found out about me and B. I think we're in jail."

"Dragons have jails?"

"It feels like one. They don't know what to do about us."

"Michael, I'm sorry to tell you this, but the king of Wentinworth is holding you responsible for what happened on his land. Every mage in the room spoke highly of you and tried to convince him this was an accident and a mistake, but he is asserting his right to avenge his people. Wentinworth will lead the charge into the Netherworld."

"Let me guess: just ascended to the throne and needs to justify why he's in power and not one of the other families."

"The king of Wentinworth has been in power for less than a year, after his uncle died without an heir."

"How did I know. Don't let them charge. At least wait until we can talk."

"We've already been instructed to lower the barrier in Wentinworth."

"What? How?"

"With enough atoms of one type collected in on place, we can do it from our side."

"In the swamp?"

"We have studied the substance you described. We know what it is, and we are making enchanted armor to repel it. If all goes well, the soldiers will walk on dry land."

"Era, this is horrifying! They want to send their own soldiers into the *Netherworld*!"

She looked around, as if making sure nobody on her side was listening. "Michael, I have a feeling preparing nine nations for war will be a long, drawn-out process. Hopefully by the time everything is ready, the ruling families will have lost the appetite."

"Make the nobles fight in it themselves. They'll lose their stomachs quickly."

"Right now we only have enough of the right type of atom to break one barrier. Finding more will take time, but it will happen. Could take years."

I laughed. "So the war isn't supposed to end?"

"Eighty-five years of relative peace has left a gaping hole in the coffers of several kingdoms."

"I knew it. Hirinda proved peaceful research could be profitable, but everyone falls back on war. Well, I'm glad I didn't get my hopes up for rejoining human society. I think I would have requested a hawk or an eagle. Some kind of body that would allow me to fly away from all this human shit."

"I would have gladly performed the soul transfer myself. You seem pretty happy with B. Are you?"

"I think he's going out of heat. I'm not sure what will happen now, but we're getting along. I sort of have to be with him, but I like being with him. He has this happy, carefree way about him. Reminds me of my early years as a hired sword. I wish I could talk to him."

"A happy relationship with another man. Perhaps you should tell the Church why my proper marriage failed but your unholy bond works."

"Scent! B smells so good, and I know he likes my scent as well. Maybe every dragon binds together that way. No forcing two people who shouldn't be together to live with one another for the sake of land. They sniff each other's junk[42] and they know they're right for one another."

She chuckled. "I almost envy you. I would never choose the married life again."

"Think how much better things would be if nobody had to marry. If two people *wanted* to be together. No politics. No land grabs. No more parents using their children to get more land or livestock. Era... if you don't mind me asking, what happened to your husband?"

I swore I could see her smile. "My late husband ignored me most of the time. Whenever he talked to me, I could hear the resentment in his voice. He would have sent me away if his family hadn't also pressured him to marry. Then he started inviting people over, and he would provoke me into arguments. I knew what he was doing. He was trying to make it look like I was a horrible woman. I feared he would try to kill me. Someone in the village also saw what was happening and offered to teach me some spells. She taught me one that let me sleep only when he slept. After months of being awake with him, sure enough I woke up in the middle of the night and heard him get out of bed and fetch the ax from outside. When he brought it in, I waited for him to swing it down on the bed. I used a deflection spell, and the ax cracked his skull."

"Ouch. You'll be happy to know there doesn't seem to be such an imbalance here. The men don't have power over their wives. No husband would be able to kill his wife and make it look like she had it coming. Everyone has claws and

---

42 The original word was *forests*. "Junk" did not replace it until the 1600s, when shaving one's pubic hair became fashionable. Most surviving sources use the modern term.

teeth, and the men and women are the same size. Well, except me. Nobody's my size."

"I'm liking this dragon society more and more. I'm afraid I won't be able to contact you very much from now on. The mages in Hirinda are being monitored now. I'm only here because I insisted our spy needed to know what's happening."

"Please, Era, beg them for more time. I am certain B knows what those giants are for. Once I learn the language, we can talk to the dragons. Imagine that. *Talking* to *dragons!*"

"I don't think anybody is interested in hearing from them."

"Right, sure, all the stories. Has anybody actually seen a dragon firsthand, or do we just hear about them in taverns from people who claim their uncles saw one? I don't think there are any places where dragons can enter our world."

"What's your point?"

"We know nothing about them, and the royal families want to send soldiers in to kill them! Please give me more time."

"We are still preparing. I will make an effort to reach you again before the conflict begins. In the meantime, the more you learn, the better."

"Thanks for not forgetting about me."

She flickered and faded away. I had a hard time believing B could not hear any of that. I still had trouble believing Era could hear me even though I never spoke.

War. I couldn't help but feel responsible for it, even though from what Era had told me, the noble families had been itching to go to war for years. Some needed to justify their position. Others needed an excuse to raise taxes, others wanted new territory to conquer and plunder to fill their own purses. I tried to remind myself these people would have done this whether I found giant dragons and accidentally dropped a goo swamp on someone's farmland or not. The feeling that I had caused it still simmered in my mind. I wanted to take flight and leave this place, but B would not budge. Whatever the dragon mages had told him brought him down.

I don't know how long we lay on that platform above the ocean. The wind brought no scents our way, so either nothing existed within flying distance, or we had some kind of magical barrier around us. This whole place could have been an illusion, too.

Entire kingdoms were about to send people into the Netherworld to kill dragons. I had given them the information they needed about what to expect while in here. I had given them a reason to be scared enough to make a preemptive strike. At least three reasons. Thousands of lives could be lost, and here I lay.

At some point, the land turned yellow again, and then the yellow faded, and we were back in our tower, curled up in the bowl. The sun had set again, so we might have been in jail for one day or twenty.

Now I melted into vapor and began to drift up over the bowl. As the closest thing I had to sleep, I looked forward to this. At least I didn't have to be bored while I watched B sleep.

Then B rolled to his feet and sat upright. He was awake, and the look on his face was something I had never seen on him before. He was *determined*.

I began drifting. I flowed straight to the blue dragon. Into his face. Then everything went black. It stayed black for a long time, but I had no sense of time. And then I began to run, as in a dream, and to either side of me I saw flashes of my life. Helping father set up shop. Helping mother keep track of my sister. Chasing my sister when she wandered off a bridge and into the city. Kissing my brother... Enticing him to pull his dick out... Sucking my brother's dick...

I saw school. Barely had time to attend; family was always moving and father and mother needed so much help. I remembered a few schoolmasters. I remembered sitting in one place for me was almost impossible. One man had to smack me with a stick so I'd give attention to the math lesson. If I could go back and kiss that man now, I would.

I hated our wagon. I hated my father's unending quest to find things to take with him and sell. I hated the constant, nagging worry about having enough money. I fucking hated the moving around. I ran into a city and never looked back.

From here, memories bled into one another. I kept running, and to my side I saw myself chopping wood, herding sheep, tying up horses at an inn.

I met someone who set me on my path in life.

Training. Apprenticeship. I did my first job on my own, and I finally had income.

Now memories collided like two rivers.

I emerged from an egg.

I tore into a carcass my mother dropped for me.

I watched another dragon laying eggs, and I became determined to lay eggs, too, so I found some and slipped them under my tail and won't mother be so proud of me. Then one of the eggs broke inside me.

I saw a massive, muscular dragon. I followed him for hours, just watching his arms and shoulders. I walked under him and watched his stomach and chest pulse above me. I had never seen a dragon whose muscles bunched up as he walked. Why didn't all dragons look like this?

Mother pushed me out of the tower, and my wings flapped until I learned to fly. Most dragons learned how to fly this way. The ones who did not fell to their deaths. I watched a few of them fail to take flight.

Once I could fly, I was on my own. I took stones from numerous people and helped mend and clean the towers and paths and bridges.

I visited temples. I watched the giant dragons for hours at a time. I seemed to be the only one interested in coming to these places. I touched my slit. I spent days on top of those dragons, just taking in the scope and the size.

I fucked around with so many people. Sex outside of heat cycles was enough, but I couldn't wait to find out how it felt when my scent became full.

Information came to me, as it does in dreams: all dragons who go into heat live in the wilderness until it passes so the scent doesn't agitate everyone in the city.

A very rare chance the heat would never pass. I hoped it would happen to me.

I waited in a cave for my heat either to pass, or for someone to notice it and venture inside. I figured my scent projected what I was interested in, and I hoped somebody would meet it. I had planned to go out and seek someone else who might be in heat and receptive to my advances when some creature from the Other Place attacked.

And then *he* appeared.

The dragon of my dreams. The image and scent of maleness I had always desired.

The two rivers mixed together so thoroughly I couldn't tell the fresh water from the salt water. I watched myself. I heard myself speaking. I understood the dragon's words but not mine. I understood my words but not the dragon's.

The rivers began to separate, and I discovered I had a mouth again.

The bone tower faded into view. My vapor had separated from B, and now I floated before him. He later told me part of the vapor took on solid form. I was a dragon mask floating in front of B. The rest of me was just a green fog.

B grunted and huffed. Now he made sense. "You fucked your brother?"

My mouth and throat suddenly knew how to respond. "You shoved eggs up your ass?"

B shot fire over my face. I still couldn't laugh the way he did, so I said "*hah.*"

Then B stood up and regarded me. I had no body. I just floated. "It worked! I should have known going to others would be a waste of time! I think I'm starting to understand how to control this, and now I know what's happening. I finally know your name." He tried to say it, but he couldn't wrap his tongue around any of the sounds.

I also tried to pronounce his name, but even with this tongue and mouth I couldn't do it. "You are one perverted bastard and you are also the best lay I've ever had."

He leaned forward and bumped noses with me. "I didn't know what was happening. You just... became whatever I wanted. I didn't know until later I was in control of it, and now I think I have control. You really like it?"

Now I exerted some control. I pushed myself forward and rubbed snouts with him. He rubbed back. The vapor formed an arm and part of a neck. I reached up. My arm wasn't connected to anything, but somehow I had control of it. I held his hand, and he felt my neck, running his fingers over the muscles. Even now, he made my disconnected limbs thick and rippling. Lots of veins this time.

"I understand now," B continued. "I was worried I was forcing you to be something for me, but you asked for it, and then you invited me to feel you up and make you bigger and, and, and I... I..."

"Everything you do to me feels incredibly good."

"You really do come from the Other Place. Only young dragons can go there. Everyone else is too big."

"I have so many questions."

"So do I! Let's go where no one will hear us." He spread his wings and began walking to the door, but then he paused. "Wait. We don't have to go anywhere."

My mask-like face and neck dissolved. I funneled back into B's skull, and this time things did not go black. I saw our alcove through his eyes, and he walked us to the bowl and lay inside it.

This will be faster.

"How much of my life did you see?"

Flashes. Lots of them. Let's start with that weapon you had. I saw you changing its shape, and I figured the same thing was happening now, but what was it?

I deduced he had missed the conversations with Era, so I tried to open myself up to him. I pictured that first sleep in the cave, when Era had appeared to me and explained what they had been doing, and how the weapon worked. When I did, I sensed B behind my eyes, too.

That's beyond anything we have. We always suspected people in the Other Place had magic, too. I'm... I'm sorry I broke your weapon.

"I'm sorry I stabbed you. They hired me to test it. Poke and run. That's all I had to do."

And now you're the weapon, and you're bound to me. This... This has been amazing.

"I fucking love it. Make me as big as you want. Call me dad, too, if you like. I've been called that a couple times in my life."

You caught me while I was in heat, so that's all I've been thinking about. I was worried you weren't along for the ride until you started it. You're the first from Other Place

I've ever met. I can't remember any stories of us being able to talk to anyone from there.

"So please help me. I don't understand most of what I'm seeing."

I can't begin to understand your life either. I don't know where to begin.

"Let's talk about those giant dragons. What are they? Who are they? How did they get there?"

Oh, those. The mages created them centuries ago.

"We have records of magical places going back thousands of years. Those places."

The mages told us they'd have some effects in Other Place. Time stretching, distance distortion. Those dragons are preserved in a magical state. The stones are increasing their size to make new entry points for us.

"Why? Why would any of you want to go to Other Place?"

To get more magic. There are no places dragons can enter that world and retrieve magical artifacts. We've built our whole civilization on magic, and there isn't enough of it for everyone.

"Why does there need to be?"

Why shouldn't there be?

"I mean that you're the biggest thing around. You can hunt everything, live anywhere, you seem to fear nothing. What's so important about magic?"

Magic builds the towers we live in. Magic makes the paths pleasing to our feet. Soon, magic will bring peace here.

"Peace? Is there war?"

Remember I took you hunting? We have a horrid relationship with the other people. The gryphons. The akeptrox. We hunted them for thousands of years before we realized they could talk. Now we know everyone can talk. We have culture and cities, and... and... And yet we still have to eat.

"They're all people?"

Yes, and we have to hunt them. I feel bad hunting them. We all do. When we open the barriers, we'll be able to sustain ourselves with magic. We won't have to hunt anyone anymore. If it works, they won't have to hunt anything either. If I'm right about your Place, you are fortunate your food can't talk. Your world must be so much more peaceful.

"What exactly do you need from Other Place?"

More stones that can be shaped to fit in our horns. You saw us in the town. Only a few sustenance stones to go around. We can't make enough stones for everyone to be capable of magic. We all want to be, but there is so little magic here. We have to take turns having it. Only the mages can do the complicated spells. I used magic to peek into your mind, but it didn't make much sense. I got a few tastes and smells and images. I made you taste that fermented fruit-water when you sucked my jizz. I hoped you'd know I was trying to understand you. This person you talk to. How can she reach you here?

"Something about projecting herself to areas of high magic concentration. Our kind of magic. So... those blobs we sang to. What are they?"

They feed the towers.

"Feed?"

These are living creatures.

"Of bone?"

The bone is on the outside. Under the bones are nerves and hearts and lungs. We all have to help feed our city, or it's back to living among trees that are trying to cut through our skin. Does everyone in your Place[43] not want to become a mage?

"No. I had no interest in it."

Why not? Magic is the solution to all problems.

---

43 Not all manuscripts capitalize this usage of the word.

"Where I come from, it's caused more problems than solved."

That's hard to believe.

"So the giants will open ways between the two worlds. Do you have any idea what else is on the other side? The people who will attack you there?"

We know there are people in the Other Place, but we can't talk to them. When we get more magic, we will. The mages didn't believe me when I told them you were from the Other Place.

"But they know we have a connection."

I had to tell them. When the teaching spell failed, I had to show them. They're not sure what to make of you. I'm surprised they let us come home. I have to hide you, even now. One of them is probably watching us.

"I don't blame them. We did sort of break the barrier."

I got carried away! I was so happy my family liked you, and you asked me to make you bigger earlier, so I wanted to show you something I've done since I was little. I used to visit those giants and rub off on them. Dragons that size... I was the only one I knew who came out[44] just being around them. I thought you might want to share that with me and then—and then the world broke! I was so sorry—I knew I couldn't keep you to myself anymore—I had to talk to someone about this.

"I remember seeing you on one of the giants, rubbing yourself. That makes sense now. Wait, your family liked me? How? I can't even speak!"

Your scent. It's impressive. Everyone in the city thinks it is. Not all of us can speak the other's language, and even some dragons have languages we can't share. That's another reason we need more magic. We want to talk to everyone.

---

44 That is, came out of his slit. M rendered the expression literally.

All of the other people here can speak but we don't have enough magic.

I tried to reach out to Era—tried to tell her I needed to talk to her immediately.

All right, all right, you can feel them,[45] but here's the deal. I take your cum. You don't take mine. With a little luck, you'll go back to normal soon.

You like my arms. I like feeling them get bigger, especially when someone is touching them. It still helps me feel real.

Weird that I like my body more as a quadruped. I think I've learned to appreciate how B sees me.

Keep feeling my stomach. B can tell what you're touching.

I don't think this body could exist in nature. B definitely likes what you're telling him. So do I. It's been fun, being this large among men. It's even more fun being huge among dragons.

---

45 *He's been growing for hours. A little at a time. His muzzle now rests between his chest muscles. His arms are thrice as thick as his head. His thighs are twice as thick as his arms, and even his cock looks similarly muscular.*

SESSION 9

Settle in.[46] I don't want to break during this part.

B had flown us to one of the other giants, and now he separated me from his body. I stood next to him, thrice his mass and only slightly taller, gazing up at the dragon that looked to be the size of a hundred cities.

"I wondered why you were so scared when you saw one for the first time."

"I didn't know what I was looking at. The scale of these dragons. I'm still having a tough time grasping anything this huge."[47]

"These dragons will save us. They will create peace."

Even with my new skill at his language, I still couldn't pronounce his real name.

"B, the people in Other Place know about this, and they think you're going to invade."

His neck curled. "Invade? Why would we do that? We can only eat things of this world."

"Enough mass will push natoms and atoms together, and the natoms win. They did over that farm. You saw them. They became something else."

---

46 *I called him. He heard me. He fucked me all night. I don't care what happens to me. I don't care if the scales are spreading. I don't care that the world seems to be dimming. He's looking at me. He knows how I feel. He knows what I want. He will give it to me.*

47 *I do not want to go back to normal. I will convince him to give me more.*

"The mages told me that happened because of us. Too much too fast. That's why these bodies are growing gradually. Weaken the barrier slowly so when it breaks, it won't be a flood. All we want is magic."

"Rocks. You want rocks."

"Rocks, gems, plant life."

"The sustenance stones. What are they made of?"

"I don't know how you would describe them, but they're some of the rarest magical pieces. You smelled a few of them in the city."

"I did?"

"Think back, M. Here. Let me remind you."

Relieving to know he couldn't pronounce my real name either. I turned to vapor and swirled into B's skull, exiting just as I entered and reforming on his other side.

"I'm getting better at this," B said. "I think I can hold you in any shape I want now."

"Sawdust, copper, steel, olive oil."

"Is that what you call them?"

I couldn't stop laughing as I told him "Your magic is my every day life! Era won't believe this is all you want. The monarchs won't believe it."

"Why wouldn't they? Your sword was made of pieces of swamp and air and dragon urine and a few other things."

"All this just to get some wood and sandstone!"

"I'm sure your mages would be happy to trade your worthless materials for ours."

"It's not that simple. Kings and queens are about to invade this place. It will be an endless war."

"I don't understand why they would. Magic can solve all problems, and you have magic in abundance over there."

"B, we need to be prepared for the worst. Maybe there's another way to bring down the barrier. Can't you do it on a smaller scale?"

"It will only be large enough for one or two adults to go through at a time. This *is* small."

"Fuck, how can we convince them they don't need to invade? No matter what I think of, it still looks like the Netherworld is coming. They only know the stories about monsters and demons and killer plants and magical objects. They will never believe dragons are intelligent and only want to trade for some rocks."

I looked at him, scented the air coming off him.

"You must be out of heat. I don't want to lick your slit anymore."

"Yes, I'm coming out of it. I still might want to from time to time, but it won't be as much as now."

"Too bad. I'm still in heat."

"I can tell."

"Are you making that happen?"

"Maybe. I've always had a fantasy of being hunted down and fucked, and that pushes me into heat."

I growled and nudged him on the shoulder. My claws grew. My horns grew. My vision had a strange halo around it, and I figured my eyes were now glowing red. Those lava veins I had earlier surfaced all over my skin again as my muscles expanded.

I turned and lowered my head, stalking.

He took off running, flapping his wings sloppily and just barely managing to take to the air. I spread my wings, grunting as my height rose a yard and my arms inflated. I took off. My scales began changing color, and I glanced down at my claws. They were still growing and also changing to white.

In mid-air, a wave rushed through my body, and I had to adjust my flight as I swelled. Other things were happening to me, too. Things I couldn't see. B would later tell me he made spines grow out of my back and on the back of my arms. He gave me some on my face as well. I must have looked demonic.

B led us over the giant dragon, which produced its own climate. I saw clouds hanging over him, and I swear I saw lightning moving between them. B flew straight for those clouds and vanished inside them.

I thought I might lose him, but I had yet to use my senses. I saw him through the clouds, the heat he gave off. When the clouds obscured that, I swear I saw his scent. Just like the hand print, my eyes now saw his scent through the clouds. I stayed on him, observing my arms getting bigger, my chest bulging, my forelegs filling out more and more.

My wings had grown far out of proportion, and they propelled me forward like a minnow in a river. I overtook B in a few more strokes and caught him, and when I realized how large he had made me, I almost panicked. My arm alone was as thick as his whole body. I wrapped both of them around him, thrust him against my chest, and let us both fall.

He struggled, searching for a way to break my grip, but I flexed every muscle in my body and held him against me. When we fell through the clouds, the giant dragon slowly came up to meet us. He must have been the size of a continent, and we were careening down toward the hips.

B gasped and tried to worm away, scratching and clawing. I held my hand over him, and I just now noticed my claws were as long as his arms.

I flapped and rolled us over. Holding him felt as easy as a bundle of flowers, and I streamlined my body, picking up speed all the way down to the surface and slowing down gradually so I wouldn't crush him on landing.

I slid to a stop, my claws not even making a mark on the giant's hide. B tried to escape, and I ran my hand across his chest, drawing blood. I loomed over him and growled. He stood under me, pinned down by my chest and one arm around his neck.

I came out of my slit. I growled again and angled my hips. My legs were so thick I had to make a wide stance just to crouch low enough to mount him.

B's heat scent came back, and my hips bucked without me telling them to. I bucked until I found his hole and then shoved it in all the way. I relaxed my grip on him and concentrated on fucking him.

He ran, slipping out all the way, leaving me hanging. I had not expected that; I figured once being caught pushed him into heat again, he'd stay put, but now he ran across the giant's scales. I gave chase, though moving with all these muscles pushing against each other made me feel slow and clumsy. Just a feeling though; I caught up to him in only a few strides.

B had started to take flight. I reached up and smacked him out of the air with one hand. He fell, hit the scaly ground, and rolled. I jumped on top of him and pinned his wings down. Now on his back, B had a clear look at me, and if I thought he'd been in heat a moment ago, his scent exploded now.

I ran my hand across him again, making shallow wounds on his chest and stomach. Blood mixed with heat excited me. I growled again and rose higher, making him look at these muscles in motion—not just decoration, but being used to pin him down and fuck him.

I raised my hips and shoved my cock all the way in. He lay sprawled out, helpless and hard, drinking in the sight. He struggled, and I had to restrain him. He watched the muscles roll around under my skin as I held him. He watched my stomach and legs bulge as I thrust. No gentle giant this time. He wanted to feel caught, and I fucked him like an animal.

When I finished, so did he, and I lapped it up. When I pulled out, I did not let him go. I lay on top of him, making him feel my weight. He stared up at me, completely spent.

"That was fun."

I rubbed snouts, being careful not to poke him with any of my new spikes. "I remember seeing a muscular dragon in your memory. Was that real? Do dragons like this even exist?"

"Oh yes! It doesn't happen often, but they get this big."

"Who was that giant you followed?"

"His name was..." Sorry, I can't pronounce what he said with this tongue. P will do. "P. He lived here when I was little. I had such a crush on him growing up. I used to follow him all day. I watched him from the tower. Just watching him walk around. They often asked him to move heavy things, and I wanted to feel him up so bad. I only met one other person like him. I hoped someone like that would find my scent appealing."

"You wanted to be caught and captured so he could use you whenever he wanted."

"It's just as good as I imagined. Is this what you want?"

"I want to be whatever you make me."

"Please use me."

I laughed and said, "I think shoving those eggs in your ass as a kid really fucked you up."

"I was drawn to these things even as a child. It only got stronger as I grew up."

"Something strange is happening to your scent. B, it's starting to..."

"That's another fantasy of mine. Sometimes a dragon's scent can push another dragon into heat. I think... I think..."

I breathed B's scent in. It smelled so good it went straight to my groin. My slit didn't just drip; lube burst out in a flood.

"I'm making that happen, am I?[48]" B asked.

I lay on him, soaking him. "Keep making it happen. This is fun." I liked his snout. "And I like you."

I noticed my spines had retracted. I scooped him up and rolled to my back so now he lay on top of me, muzzle nestled in my chest.

We lay on top of the sleeping giant. B didn't sleep, but I tried. As much as I had done, I didn't feel tired, and without that break in the day, I didn't know what to do.

Then I heard Era's voice. "Michael?"

I turned my head and looked all around but could not see her projection. This time I spoke aloud. "Era? Where are you?"

"Michael, they're invading now."

"Now?!"

I rolled to my side, setting B down, and rose to my feet, still looking for her. Finally I noticed her standing on one of the scales.

"I thought you'd delay them!"

"The king of Wentinworth issued a decree to round up people, run them through the courts, and convict them of a crime. Loitering, idleness, dissent. I hear as many as twenty crimes carry a sentence of conscription in the military, with a pardon upon safe return."

"Round up?"

"Towns are encouraged to gather the poor, the vagrants, dissenters. Other domains are doing something similar. The public decree calls the soldiers brave men who will avenge and protect their country."

---

48 Many sources use the more modern contraction *aren't I?* This sentence construction did not exist in M's time and is a later change.

"What about that protective armor and weapons? Have you made any?"

"None, and that's the point. Seems the monarchs are using this opportunity to rid their countries of surplus population. No coincidence the monarchs all passed quiet decrees making it illegal to sleep in public spaces, or speak against the townmaster or any officer of the crown, whether in the past or present. People are being arrested for past crimes they'd already served penalties for."

"Where are they coming in?"

"Where the slime leaked into our world. They'll be approaching from the north. I'm committing treason telling you this, Michael, but I felt the need to inform you in case you can do anything on your side to stop this."

"Era, I know what the giants are for! They're creating breaches in the barrier so they can come through and find ordinary rocks and pieces of wood! They want everyone to be a mage, but they can't get materials. That's all they want! They're not invading! They want sawdust and sandstone! Tell the monarchs to call it off!"

"Did they teach you about the Bossford mine in school?"

"No."

"Gold mine discovered at the top of the world. The monarchs did the same thing then, too, rounded up all the dissenters and poor people and sent them to work it and hopefully never to return, and those that survived would have been molded into model citizens, willing to work and loyal to the crown. I remember reading about this happening again when the Lisi islands were discovered. They told the people they sent brave people out to colonize the land and tame it for the glory of the crown. In reality they just shipped their criminals and homeless to die."

"This is—! How can they get away with it?"

"They are the monarchs. This is how they deal with society's problems. The army of conscripts is marching right now. Many will likely die on the march, but expect thousands to come through. Once they're dead, they'll send in real soldiers with real equipment for the real war that will no doubt be profitable for the people making the weapons, and the mages who have to enchant them. Michael, I don't want to work for the military. Please. I must leave. I still—"

She stopped and looked to the side. Her projection flickered.

"I have informed our spy to leave the area. You do realize shackles won't hold me."

Her shade vanished, and I turned to B. He was staring at me, and I had returned to my normal form at some point, green scales and no lava veins.

"Did you hear any of that?"

B sat on his haunches. "I can only hear you speaking. Was that your mage in the Other Place?"

"We need to go. I'll explain on the way."

I led him out of the cave, propelled us through the ocean, and made a line straight for the swamp. B had a difficult time understanding what the monarchs were doing. I had to explain what a poor person was, and I believe the words I used were something to the effect of if you fall behind and don't have any money, you can't do anything, so they throw you out.

B asked why someone doesn't just give them money so they can get started again.

I told him if you have no money, you have no place to live, and nobody will want to hire someone who doesn't have roots.

"If no one will let them work, how are they supposed to earn money?"

"I don't know."

"So being without money is a crime in Other Place?"

"In a word, yes."

"Why can't they go and live in their own cave and hunt for themselves?"

"The noble families own all the land. They must pay to live on it or be arrested by the police and locked away."

"Where they can't earn money? This is confusing."

"B, we need to stop this army from coming in, and I think I know how. We'll break the barrier, now, before they can, and I'll block the way."

"Block? What do you mean?"

I picked up speed. My internal map took me over the singing sands, the living hedge maze, the deadly vines, and then I felt another dragon presence tugging me. The swamp came in sight, and I led us down to where I remembered. I saw some familiar-looking trees and petrified remains of distorted human beings sticking out of the slime.

I landed right where I had been before, ankle deep in the muck.

"Make me grow, B. As big as you can. Big enough to open the barrier."

B was shaking as he looked around, and I could smell he wanted to see me that big again but he remembered what happened last time. "You're sure you want to do that?"

"This is worse than a pointless war! This is outright murder! If I can stop it, I fucking will! I just need to be bigger than the army! Bigger than the kings and queens! Bigger than the damn noble houses! Bigger than all the fucking people who want this to happen!"

My height rose half a yard. My arms stretched and filled out to match, and my tail lengthened. The surge made my cock burst out of my slit.

I looked at him and laughed as my neck reached another yard upward, and the rest of me bulged out. I adjusted my stance.

"I was worried it would be difficult for you."

He walked up to me and rested his face on my chest, looking up my neck. "I'm so happy you want this, too."

I wrapped an arm around him as my muscles expanded, and he became squeezed between my chest and my arm. He closed his eyes. Right about then, I felt something happen. A dam burst. Waves moved through me so fast I barely had time to breathe, much less adjust my stance. I let go of him as my arm thickened. I didn't want to crush him if it grew too much. Just as I let go, my height shot up about three yards and my arms and legs doubled in thickness.

Of course he'd make sure my muscles grew out of proportion.

The sky looked so far away I couldn't imagine being able to reach the clouds. I spread my legs farther apart. I wanted to peek down my stomach, but my chest had expanded so large I couldn't move that way anymore, so I reached up with a hind foot and felt my underside. Just then another wave, and my stomach thickened, spreading to my legs, then up my chest and down my arms and finally up my neck.

I reached up and felt my neck as my height rose. New muscles appeared under the scales. Old ones thickened. B liked how it looked. I sure liked how it felt.

I planted all four feet in the slime as I widened during another rush. I stood thrice as tall as B. He was sitting, feeling himself. He would later tell me he wasn't hard simply from watching these muscles in motion. He had been afraid we wouldn't get along. That we'd be magically bound together and grow to despise one another and I'd want to go home. It's what tends to happen when fantasy becomes reality. I know. I met the woman of my dreams once and it turned into a nightmare. That I enjoyed this as much as he did must have been proof of divine intervention for him.

I lowered my neck down to the muck and inhaled his arousal. I felt my dick dip into the slime. It reached my chest, and I guessed it had become as thick as my arm.

"This feels just as good as it looks," I told him. I think I could've finished just from finally being able to tell him that.

He licked my neck and then climbed to his hind legs and embraced it as it thickened. The muscles bulged out, spreading his arms apart. I licked his dick while I was down here. Damn, he tasted good. I widened my stance while a couple ripples ran down my legs, stretching them out. My neck rippled again, and I rose to full height. B dropped and beheld me as I rose above the trees.

My shoulders looked like prairie hills carved by thin rivers, the gouges between them so deep I don't think anyone could have climbed them.

I spread my wings and looked at them. The muscles running up them looked as thick as my arms, and as my height climbed another yard, the clouds moved closer.

I looked down and noticed a few two-headed canines standing next to B. A couple other gryphons came near and were staring up at me beside B. They sniffed B's cock briefly before turning to look at me.

I noticed other animals or people filtering in through the swamp. Finally I saw some creatures in flight besides dragons. I had an audience. I laughed to myself, wondering what I should expect.

My height shot up a few more yards, and I widened my stance, releasing a grunt and a moan as my muzzle stretched out. The sound of me growing now seemed to carry across the entire swamp.

My dick peeked between my pecs. I couldn't see my hands anymore, but I could see the tip, and the barbs flared whenever a growth spurt washed through it. It kept up with my body plus a little more, just like my muscles.

I had grown high enough to see a large part of the swamp from over the trees, and I saw myself in the muck. My arms and chest resembled the foothills of the Great Range. I leaned over to get a better look at what B was doing to me, and I saw down my flanks how the abdominal muscles ringed my stomach and joined with the muscles at my back. They grew, and the growth spread down my arms, deepened the valleys between the muscles, spread my fingers, and then raised my height another three yards.

I noticed the Judges stepping out of vertical tears in the air. I tried to compose myself as my dick thickened and brushed against my arms. I could hear B explaining what was going on. I was afraid I'd have to defend myself against whatever magical attacks they threw at me, but whatever B was telling them must have been convincing, for they just stood there and watched.

I must have had half the people in the Netherworld watching me now. I wondered where they had been before. B must have wanted an audience this time. Now that our secret was out, he wanted to prove it could be useful. I had an internal sense of direction, so I turned around, angling my body east-west so anyone coming from the North would see me in profile. This also meant B saw me in profile, and now everyone had a full view of my dick.

It thickened and grew past my chest muscles. I couldn't see my feet, but I could see my dick now. My legs grew, and I rose a few more yards.

I felt my tail stretching, and I swung it, taking down a few dozen trees. As the next wave stretched my torso out and thickened it, I roared. No fire. For some reason B couldn't give me that, and I would later learn this put me at a disadvantage in dragon society, but everything else more than made up for it.

This next wave felt different. Before, it had been passive growth—as if growing bigger was my normal state, and B simply put a cork in that. This time, I felt B actively making me larger.

The wave ripped through me, and my arms doubled in size, followed by my torso and legs and then tail. My height must have leaped twenty yards in a single motion. My cock had not grown this time, but the rest of me had, and judging by my reflection in the slime, it ended up being proportional.

Another one of these deliberate spurts swelled up in me, and I rose to my hind legs, roaring as it swept me. When I crashed down to the swamp, I had risen another ten yards, and my legs were so thick they squeezed my cock. Even my forelegs put pressure on it, to say nothing of my chest, which stuck so far out it cast shadows of its own.

I growled and roared as the waves increased. I looked to my side and saw B straining. A couple of the dragon mages were shining some sort of magical light on him, either examining or helping. B wasn't just letting me grow on my own now. He pushed me higher. Wider. He had taken control, and now I had risen halfway to the clouds.

Now the waves felt different. The best way I can describe it is drawing back the bow and then releasing the arrow. B did that. He drew back, built up, and then released the wave all at once, but even bigger than the smaller ones would have been.

I had a moment to breathe while he drew back, and I observed the crowd. Beetles to me now, and I still had a long way to go.

I clenched my teeth and rose to my hind legs again. This time I held onto my dick as B released, and I think I rode my dick as it thrust forward across the swamp, and I expanded to match it.

I panted again and looked around. The clouds had come closer. The people below had become ants. The swamp had become a flat sheet of tar to me, and my hands barely noticed the muck.[49]

I could feel the bowstring drawing back. I braced my-self and waited for it. Moments later, I heard wingflaps, and someone landed on my head.

"We have a problem, M," B said.

"What?"

"The mages are telling me someone on the other side is trying to weaken the barrier, too. This may be too much. You might cause more harm."

"Era told me they had a way to do this from their side. It will come down hard no matter what we do. I trust the soldiers are a safe distance away."

"I hope you know what you're doing."

"I spent years of my life watching how battles go. I know where they'll be. I need my human voice back. Can you give that to me?"

"I think I can."

"Good, because..."

My next words became a choked mumble as little waves hit my throat. Now the big drawback B had been making snapped, and I shot up fifty yards. Thankfully my dick wasn't so big I had to lie on it, but it would make move-

---

49 *I want him to pin me in that swamp and fuck me.*

ment difficult, especially being squeezed between my legs and chest like this.

B landed on one of my pectorals. He had a flat platform to stand on—that's how far out they jutted. I practiced speaking my human words, and B kept adjusting my throat while he also drew back the bowstring.

Moments later, it snapped, and my muscles exploded outward before my height rose fifty yards. Now I saw my dick over my chest, and I rested my front half on it as I waited for the next wave and practiced my speech.

I felt it. The air around me weakening. Falling into something. From the corner of my eye, I saw the army. They had gathered a safe distance away, and I wondered if they could see me. Thousands of people, and my vision was now good enough to make out their faces even from this high up. Era was right. These were no soldiers. These were poor and destitute people forced to march to their deaths. Most did not even know how to stand in formation, much less hold a weapon. Instead of dealing with the problems in society, the nobility waited for opportune moments like this to send undesirable people to their death. No need for you to acknowledge poverty and crime and the lack of paid work and the people who can't work hard enough to pay tribute to live on the land you own or pay the debts they have to acquire just to buy the livestock they need to grow the crops you demand as tribute—just purge the country every few generations when there are too many poor people. Just send them to some distant continent to work and die. Send them to the fucking Netherworld so you don't have to look at what you are doing to people, and then keep telling the farmers and the merchants and the clergy and the wizards that you are indispensable but the people who grow your food and fight your wars are the surplus population. Finally, I could do something about the aristocracy's bullshit and tell them who the fuck needs you to own the land when thousands of people would be better off if they didn't have to surrender a chunk of their harvest just so you can keep your lavish mansions furnished.

The air flickered, and I began to see farmland through the swamp all around me. I surged upward again. My body bulged outward. My dick jutted forward. I lowered my forelegs to confirm I could still stand.

A few more flickers and flashes later, and the air yielded around me. I swear the air itself collapsed, and behind the curtain, I saw the soldiers standing on farmland, and I stood in the exact place I had been when B and I broke the barrier the first time.

Swamp slime and farmland mixed. The trees caught in the transition changed into twisted, distorted forms of themselves, and then everything calmed down.

I looked out over the soldiers. I smelled their fear from here. I smelled some of them had wet themselves. B dropped from my chest and soared over and up, perching on my crown.

I lifted a leg and took a step. My dick mowed down dozens of trees and plowed the soil. I lifted another leg and took another step to the soldiers. Some of them were trying to run, but most just held still and beheld the sight coming for them through the barrier.

I stepped through. The human land looked so dim to me now, and a single claw of mine dwarfed ten soldiers. I made a show of pounding the ground as I approached them. Some were trying to run, but enough of the soldiers tried to show loyalty, or maybe they believed if they fought valiantly and survived they'd be pardoned upon return, so the army as a whole stood still. Some even drew their unenchanted swords, which nobody had told them would not work against anything from the Netherworld.

I took slow, plodding steps toward them. The quakes I made prevented anyone from moving. I turned and dropped my dick in front of them as I curled my tail around the whole army, trapping them. I used my tail to push them like insects closer to my dick. When the army had untangled themselves, I opened my mouth.

"The crown sent you to your deaths. Your king wants you to die. Don't bother fighting."

Some of the people had drawn swords and were stabbing my dick. Their swords did not even pucker the flesh. Eventually they realized the futility of their actions and backed away from me. I made some high-pitched noises.

"I'm here to tell you what the Netherworld demands. They want olive oil! Sawdust! Talc! Pyrite! And most important of all! Quartz!"

The soldiers looked confused. I laughed with my voice.

"The Netherworld demands your most precious samples of balsa! We offer our sphinx blood in exchange for your finest, purest samples of limestone!"

People were scratching their heads through their leather and bamboo armor.

"We are willing to trade our worthless gryphon feathers for some of your precious sandstone!"

I reared up on my hind legs, giving them a chance to see my underside, just as muscular and armored as the rest of me. Then I crashed to my feet, sending a quake through their ranks and making everyone fall to the ground.

"Go back to your kingdoms and tell them what I have told you. Nobody will die. We only want your precious magical artifacts, and we hope you will use our magical artifacts to end pointless bloodshed like this. Go!"

I roared and uncoiled my tail. The soldiers as a whole took off north.

My dick inflated, all the barbs rubbing against my stomach muscles and between my chest and arms. I had to lie on it to stay upright, and it just kept sliding forward, kept rubbing against me. My cock was about twice the length of my body and just as thick, and it kept going. My hips tingled.

"B, no, no, not now, no, no, no!"

I shot a load of seed so large I drenched the entire army. Many fell again, but most somehow managed to stay up and running. The soldiers had physical proof the Netherworld did not intend to invade. I've seen jars of that seed on sale for thousands of pieces of silver. It hasn't decayed at all. B and I authenticated multiple bottles, which increased their value. I can only assume people used them for pretty specific magic. Except for one person. She sent word to me it was in her wine cellar, and it was her most cherished possession. Three merchants actually gave me a cut after they sold those bottles. I paid off a few farmers' debts with the money. Kept some coins for Netherworld magic. Silver can do so many amazing things in the land of natoms. Soul transfers, ancestor summoning, lots of complex spells involving disease warding.

Sorry. B was rolling on my head, sending geysers of fire into the air in all directions.

"I can't give you fire..."

He never finished. He was laughing too hard.

That's enough for today. I can tell you're tired.[50]

---

[50] *He met me in my quarters again. He made love to me four times. He likes my scent. I have no skin left, and my loins have vanished. I am carrying his eggs. He promised to take me with him. I can't live in human society anymore. I never belonged here. My tail is growing, even without M fucking me. I have a dragon's face. It's spreading.*

SESSION 10

B kept me that size for months. He said seeing me that large made it easy to hold me in that form. He was free. For the first time in his life, he was free to indulge himself, and he indulged. He kept making my dick bigger. He liked making my back muscles thicker while he lay on me. Being that massive and bulky was fun for me, too, and I made sure he knew it. We had a lot of time to talk.

More armies came to meet me. Other kingdoms who didn't receive word of what happened to the first army. I gave them the same performance, including the finale. Then delegates from all the kingdoms came to see me, and I repeated what I told the soldiers. They did not seem to believe me, but we had prepared for that.

B gave me my new body. This body. Only eight feet tall, green scales, walking on two legs, still obscenely muscular, but a nice compromise between my old human self and the dragon B always hoped would find his scent irresistible and fuck him day and night.

When I shrank, the barrier closed again. B and I went on a tour of the nine kingdoms and spoke on behalf of all mythic creatures. They are physically unable to speak your language, and you can't speak any of theirs, so I'm the only one who can tell you what the Netherworld wants, and I spent the next few years telling everyone exactly what the Netherworld wanted. The specific ingredients that made their magic work. Turns out they had it down to formulae as well, and it was so weird describing the exact quantities of brass or cow piss the Netherworld needed to produce this mystical effect or that hallowed ritual.

We became ambassadors to the Netherworld. B became known as a friendly dragon. Yes, the stereotype of the smiling dragon frolicking among children in a field of flowers didn't exist until we came along. We spent years preparing the nine kingdoms for the Netherworld to open up, and by the time it did, they saw the advantages of peaceful existence.

It must have been about ten years later the giant dragons on the other side reached critical size, and the Netherworld opened up. Now the kingdoms were ready, and they exchanged worthless junk for our worthless junk. Their junk was magical here, and ours made magic work there.

Era and the mages in Hirinda made a sustenance stone for B so he can live here and never have to eat. I'm told it was difficult to make and required a lot of resources for something that large. All I need to live is jizz. Oh yes, Era told me it was a flaw in the weapon's design: it wasn't a completely closed system. It would have needed to be replenished with fresh natoms from time to time. Maybe every ten years or so. They were still calculating it. Thankfully, B had a never-ending supply of fresh natoms. My body must not be entirely made of natoms, as human jizz also replenishes me. Whatever happened, it must have been the exact proportion needed for me to live in both places.

At first, B was not invested in being an ambassador in the world of atoms. He was along for the sex. Of course he was. B was a young dragon. Age doesn't work quite the same among dragons compared to humans, but relatively B was barely out of his teenage years, and I was pushing forty.

B kept himself in heat for an entire year. He loved being in heat all the time. I had to be the responsible one and drag him out of bed to come to work. It was a challenge, touring the kingdoms, speaking on behalf of the Netherworld, and then having to retreat somewhere to fuck him. His scent made me horny all the time, too. It's what he wanted, and it was fun watching noble families react to my slit dripping during royal banquets and such. They had to tolerate us, and I never let them forget it. They couldn't throw me in jail for offending them, and I think I fucked B more than once just to thank him for giving me that power over them.

I took B everywhere, and he saw entire counties living in filth and enduring famine while the rich families lived in high castles and grew fat, and why? B couldn't believe what he was seeing because it doesn't happen in dragon society. Everyone has wings. Everyone has claws and teeth. Nobody owns the forest and would send officers to punish anyone for hunting deer on the king's land, or daring to grow crops without paying tribute to the noble family who owns the land.

Gradually, he became interested. He understood we had magic but didn't know how to use it. He understood all the good we could do, so finally he let himself fall out of heat. He began participating in discussions among men, as much as he could. We went back and forth between the two worlds, B telling the other dragons what he was seeing —that their assumptions of the Other Place were not true: we weren't using magic to end suffering and conflict. Some people were using magic to increase it in others while decreasing it for themselves, and still others actively restricted magic so it could not benefit anyone but the aristocracy. Nobody in the Netherworld could believe that someplace which had magic in abundance would ever think to use it to keep millions of people in the mud while lifting one or two families out of it.

Being united in a task helped our bond. B became a diplomat himself, less afraid of the atomic world and completely invested in helping the people who lived here. Magic is the solution to all the problems, and he wanted to convince everyone of this.

We've been speaking for the dragons for forty years. Every dragon in the Netherworld is a mage now. Everyone has a sustenance stone, so they no longer have to hunt the mythical creatures. The Netherworld is at peace. I know this because I see other winged creatures in the skies now. Dragons talk to the other creatures.

Era became like a sister to us. She and her team perfected charms that allowed us to communicate with humans directly. Now those charms have been banned, and anyone in possession of one is sentenced to death. A shame. I wish you could understand B.

Era became very good friends with another dragon. A woman. Dragoness. This language doesn't have a good word for that. They're living together somewhere in the Netherworld, and she's studying dragon magic over there. She's committed to staying in the Netherworld after the barrier closes. I'm not surprised she prefers a dragon marriage to a human one.

Yes, just after the barrier opened, B and I invited humans to tour the Netherworld with us. Not royals. We didn't care about the noble families. We took ordinary people with us. They saw how dragons used magic, and as we hoped, humans began to wonder why their own society wasn't using magic to end hunger and war.[51]

---

[51] The idea culminated in the revolution of 924, and the monarchies retaliating by destroying or guarding passages to the Netherworld to protect their power. Defeated, the general population forgot what M showed them, but the Scribe's Guild preserved the spirit of revolution.

Era tried to strengthen the binding spell between us, but she has no idea what the magic is doing to us now. Mages have never been successful making another weapon like the one I had. Even refining the technique to distill natoms from atoms hasn't yielded the same result. Seems I am one of a kind.

You see, people were trying to break the binding spell between us. We began to suspect not everyone liked what we were doing. After the second time, we realized they were assassination attempts. Some noble families were funding magic research of their own, trying to find a way to take us out.

We later figured out many of the aristocratic families don't want a friendly alliance with the Netherworld. They don't want the people to be aware that things could be different—that they didn't have to settle for being farmers at the mercy of their crops—that there was no real reason to give half their harvest to the nobility so a couple privileged families could live a life of luxury while they toiled in the dirt growing the food the nobles demanded. The nobles don't want abundant magic. They want war. They want a hostile place to justify their position.

The human world is still clinging to old ways of doing things. Instead of using magic to help everyone, the royals are hoarding it for themselves while the people starve.

I've been tempted to let B make me grow into a monster that will destroy the royal families. Really, I have, but what would it solve? As soon as I turn my back, new royal families will pop up to replace them, and the same thing would happen again.

B and I will be leaving the land of atoms soon. The giant dragons are already being safely dissipated. We will join dragon society permanently after the barriers reform. Humanity will be free to do whatever it pleases. On behalf of all dragons, I express my regret that human monarchies did not follow our example and have chosen to use magic to make the divide between the nobles and the commoners even wider. I am not pleased by what I see happening to my former home.

It is my hope that recording this story will preserve these events and help explain why things are the way they are. I declare, on behalf of all people in the Netherworld, that any human who makes it into the world of natoms will find refuge there.

As for me and B, I never thought I'd find someone I'd want to settle down with, but B is that person, and not just because we're still magically bound together. I'd stay with him even if I were separated. I don't know what will happen to me when he dies, but that's still a long way off. I intend to enjoy the rest of our time together.[52]

Sometimes I miss the young B, the one that just wanted to be in heat and have a strong husband use him whenever he wanted, but I am so proud of him now. He grew into a responsible adult who cares about the wider world. Fate dropped the opportunity of a lifetime at his feet, and he picked it up and ran with it and he never stumbled. It's weird saying it, after everything I've done, but watching him grow up has been more rewarding than sticking it to the noble families all these years. Seeing him seek out lectures on human history, begging people to read history books to him, getting into debates with monarchs and professors on the significance of this battle or that royal decree. Becoming a scholar. I never would have guessed B would pursue such interests, or that I'd grow to care as well.

---

52 Other records state two of the scribes who recorded his story went with them. The fate of the first is unknown, but the other became a dragoness and bore the eggs M and B could never have on their own. We know this because her children visited the atomic world to retrieve magical objects and sought out scribes to tell the story.

Yes, I love my little blue dragon. I loved him when he was in heat and that's all he wanted to be. Perhaps we'll raise a family and visit from time to time.[53]

I don't like where this atomic society is heading, so B and I will retreat to the world of natoms.[54] We have been stockpiling magical objects, same as your royals, but we are not hoarding them.

These will be my final words as ambassador of the Netherworld. I have had a wonderful life straddling the line between human and dragon, and now I go to a world without hunger or war. I hope mankind will adjust course and sail for the same continent in time.[55]

All right, story over. I've been hard for an hour and I can't see over my chest. Who wants it?

---

[53] In reaction to this line, all noble families began hoarding magical ingredients in underground shelters in case of dragon attack past the year 924. Beginning in 1067, the nobility systematically destroyed many sources of natomic particles. This scarcity of magic drove the development of technology, leading to the creation of the printing press, the fountain pen, and the dirigible, to name but a few luxuries of the modern world.

[54] The Scribe's Guild kept their reptile traits secret and used them to identify one another, deliberately spreading them to initiate fellow revolutionaries. As technology changed literacy, the Guild changed into a covert organization dedicated to preserving M's story, and his idea for how society could be. The Guild succeeded in overthrowing the monarchies and removing the aristocracy from power in one coordinated motion across all nine kingdoms simultaneously in 1782.

[55] By 1863, the Scribe's Guild succeeded in fulfilling M's vision for humanity. Old natomic sources have been rediscovered and reclaimed. New sources were found. Magic is now abundant and is being used to end poverty and the wars of the past. The monarchies have been abolished, family names have been eliminated, everyone has dragon scales instead of skin, at least. Every family owns land and uses magic to create their own prosperity. No one is permitted to own another person's livelihood. The Guild hopes to find enough natomic mass to reopen the passages to the Netherworld and make contact again.

ABOUT THE AUTHOR

Tagenar is a size-obsessed fox, and a certified Professional Scalie Admirer.

He is the author of *Jake's List*, *Exposure*, and *Don't Call Me Coach*, all published through Furplanet. His science fiction comedy, *C C S*, is published through KTM Publishing.

He lives in Ohio. If you visit enough wine bars, you might see him actively searching for a muscular scalie to admire professionally.

All he wants in life is to be pinned under a muscle-dragon's dick. Is that really so much to ask?

furaffinity.net/user/tagenar

tagenar.sofurry.com

twitter.com/TagenarAuthor

QUESTIONS FOR STUDY GROUPS

1. M states that, consciously, the socioeconomic status of his parents compelled him to run away from home. He also states he had intimate contact with his brother. Could fear or envy of the phallus have played a part?

2. Cider is mentioned at two key points: in the tavern, in
Session 1, and during the market scene in Session 7, where
B decides to seek help from other dragons in communicat-
ing with M. What is the significance of the apple represent-
ing the seeded womb (which in this case ferments, thus
symbolically giving birth to cider) as related to M's masculine penetration and growth in the Netherworld?

3. Compare and contrast the role of marriage in M's time with the present. What can we determine about social mobility within a culture in which marriage was used primarily to obtain access to land? This land is established to hold livestock. Farmland symbolizing the womb and livestock symbolizing the phallus. What can we surmise the true purpose of land possession to be?

4. M is unable to see Era's face throughout the story. Could this be accurate, considering the limits of the magic she was using, or might he simply not remember? If the latter, could this symbolize a subconscious psychological stripping of human identity and subsequent elevation of the feminine to divine status as rescuer or spirit guide? M clearly elevates the feminine while B is envious. Discuss the implications of each reaction.

5. M neglects to mention if the giant dragons which cause the barrier between the Natomic World and the Atomic World to break down are alive or not. What can we conclude from the text of M's story? M penetrates magical barriers to meet them, the phallic protagonist entering wombs and observing developing fetuses. Do these dragon caves equate to the apple, but in the process of fermenting?

6. Throughout the text, M penetrates barriers which separate Atomic from Natomic, often with B initiating growth to facilitate this action in some form. Given the prevalence of symbolic wombs and literal phalluses, what can we conclude about the presence of the color yellow?

7. Divide into two groups. Debate the pros and cons of reintroducing the informal (thou, referring only to family relations) and the formal (you, to refer to everyone outside the family) to the language the way they were used in M's time. Would this change relationships in the present day?

8. In Session 6, M mentions pottery as a potential retirement hobby. Specifically, he mentions making bowls. Given the presence of the fermented apple as a symbol of the fertilized womb, or fulfilled desire, how might the bowl serve as a symbol of the empty womb, or unfulfilled desire?

9. M's chair, as established in Session 1, is designed to contain M in such a way that his outsized muscles appear less exaggerated while sitting. From the point of view of the old nobility, discuss the connection between the role of marriage as a means of possessing and controlling the phallus and the womb, to the subconscious desire to contain a creature of M's size and strength. Why might the nobility have sought to contain M as the subconscious symbol of the phallus, and does B represent the corresponding womb?

10. Set a timer for five minutes. Each person should draw M in both his dragon form and his bipedal dragon/human form, based entirely on what they imagined from their own reading. Compare and contrast each person's drawing. Which parts did each individual emphasize? The chest? The arms? The legs? The wings? Discuss the psychological associations with each and what formal conclusions we might draw from B's choices.

11. Examine the childhood memories B and M share in Session 8. How many of these could be considered traumatic? Are they symptoms of underlying psychological conditions, or are they causes?

12. In Session 6, the swamp substance (gooey and thick but also water-like, as described by M) is the first major intrusion of the Natomic world into the Atomic (a farmland), facilitated by M's growing presence. Does the farmland relate to the fermented apple or the empty bowl as symbols of the womb?

13. In M's time, the consumption of various herbs by way of burning and inhalation was so common it is mentioned in every children's story that survives from the time, and yet M does not mention it. What can we conclude from the omission of this obvious phallic symbol?

14. M establishes in Session 6 that dragon culture regards the scent of sexual activity as intimate, not the sight, which is why B's family was able to watch M and B copulate without being awkward or rude. Does this mean the dragons in the marketplace (Session 7) who stepped in and scented or tasted them while in the act of repeated penetration were breaching etiquette?

15. In the Netherworld, the dragon mages enter and exit at
various points of the story by creating rips or holes in the
air, symbolically entering and exiting vulvas, counterbal-
ancing M's penetrating, masculine presence in their land.
Does this explain why the dragon Judges treated him with
suspicion upon arrival, subconsciously interpreting him as
an inherent threat, only later to bear witness to his growth
and become subconsciously aroused and thus accepting of
him as a necessary component of species survival?

16. Despite the historical record of queens being effective leaders of various realms, literature throughout the land of the nine kingdoms always portrays queens as evil or cruel. M's story presents a queen who is not only benevolent, but talented (albeit absent). Why has this trope persisted in fiction?

17. In most human cultures, muscularity is considered a masculine trait, so by extension strength, endurance, and firmness are also associated with the masculine. M states that in dragon society, females are just as large as males (with himself as the unreachable exception). How would these similarities in biology affect psychology in contrast with the corresponding differences in human biology? What conclusions can we draw about B regarding why he seems to be alone in his association of exaggerated muscularity with the masculine while at the same time envious of the feminine ability to lay eggs?

18. Fire is important to dragon society in that it is both an offensive weapon (when directed at non-dragons), and an expression of laughter (when directed either at fellow dragons or empty air). Discuss possible reasons B is unable to give M the ability to breathe fire but is somehow able to give him the ability to ejaculate. Is this a limit of the experimental magic, or is B psychologically unable to grant M this basic ability due to his latent envy of the feminine? Is there symbolic significance to M as the personified phallic intrusion into the womb-like Netherworld being unable to produce fire, and does this correlate with the lack of recreational consumption of burning herbs?

19. In Session 4, M describes dragon children in the
Netherworld playing with a carpenter's hammer, treating it
as a dangerous object giving off sparks and jumping
around. Divide into teams of no more than three and discuss the hammer as a symbol of the phallus seeking an
empty bowl to pound into an apple, and how this relates to
the theme of Natomic penetration. What other objects
work as a symbol of M's masculine and thus disturbing yet
necessary presence within the Netherworld?

20. Penetration and growth lead to the breaking of confines, both physical (reality itself) as well as social (class di-
vides). What other confines does M break out of, and how
do these relate to the overarching presence of the fermented apple and the empty bowl?